C000233707

MORE THAN THIS

More Than This

Guy Adams

Photographic illustrations by
Debra Wilkinson & Guy Adams

Humdrumming Ltd.
75 Withermoor Road
Bournemouth, Dorset
BH9 2QN

This Paperback Edition 2005

First published by Humdrumming 2005

More Than This Text © 2005 by Guy Adams

Photographs © 2005 by Guy Adams & Debra Wilkinson
Cover design © 2005 by Lee Thompson
Cover 'Gregory' Model : Joe Wilkinson
Interior 'Sandra' Model : Debra Wilkinson
Dallion appears as Himself.

Guy Adams, Debra Wilkinson & Lee Thompson assert the moral right to be
established as the creators of this work.

All rights reserved. No part of this book may be used or reproduced in any
manner whatsoever without written permission from the authors, except in
the case of brief quotations embodied in critical articles or reviews.

All characters in this publication are fictitious and any resemblance to any
real persons, living or dead, is purely coincidental.

This book is sold subject to the condition that it shall not, by way of trade
or otherwise, be lent, re-sold, hired out or otherwise circulated without the
publishers prior consent, in any fom of binding or cover other than that in
which it is published and without a similar condition including this condition
being imposed on the subsequent purchaser.

Published 2005 by Humdrumming
www.humdrumming.co.uk

ISBN 1-905532-05-9
ISBN 978-1-905532-05-6

Printed and bound by JEM in the United Kingdom

The Author would like to make it clear that without Jane Warner,
this book would in no way exist, not that she would ever believe it.
(but then she is *so* old)

*To Gregory Ashe
(for services rendered).*

Other Titles by Guy Adams
Deadbeat - ISBN 1-905532-02-4
Deadbeat: Dogs of Waugh - ISBN 1-905532-14-8

Also Available
The Imagineer, by Gregory Ashe
FireEye Edition - ISBN 1-905532-01-6
SnowScape Edition - ISBN 1-905532-00-8

"To think that the spectre you see is an illusion does not rob him of his terrors: it simply adds the further terror of madness itself -- and then on top of that the horrible surmise that those whom the rest call mad have, all along, been the only people who see the world as it really is."

- *C. S. Lewis*

"Nobody here but us chickens..."

- *Dallion*

MORE THAN THIS

An
Undercurrent

The problem was in the water...

... that much was clear to any with the slightest sensitivity in these matters. It was in the out of kilter flow of the tides, the way the water crawled further and further up the beach with every wave, as if reaching out to the dry land; eager to swallow... to *consume*. Yes, the sea held all the answers, anyone with an even basic knowledge of such things would realise as much at a glance.

But then, these days, that knowledge is rare; so no one realised at all...

Not that the ripples weren't felt. Delicate thumb pricking that filtered through the subconscious of those close to the edges of reality. The young and old felt it; human existence before and after the flesh either still vaguely remembered or slowly suspected. Those nudged to the emotional brim – the euphoric and the suicidal – were aware on the edge of their laughter or tears. Most of all, hidden away from the prying eyes of outsiders in their shining white house on the cliff tops, the lunatics felt it and looked to their mother, the moon, for guidance.

As the summer months came, the holidaymakers and their much-needed money came with them. The town got on with the important business of banging out a buck in the ways it knew so well. The salt-stained streets filled with escapees from factories and offices, all eager for the rough kiss-me-quick charm of the pier and front. The beaches filled, braving the bracing wind that usually blew, whipping up mini dust devils among the flapping deck chairs and breaks. The ever present Alpine bell jangle of the ragged donkeys as they marched meaninglessly back and forth along the sand mixed with the hollow mechanical cackle of the automaton clown; rocking hysterical in its glass sentry box at the pier entrance.

The water waited through it all.

Waited for stillness.

Then the season faded. The carousels spun less frequently, the gypsies' palms became light of silver and the roar of the crowds faded like the sickly sweet smell of candyfloss borne away on cold autumn winds.

The cold crept back into the streets, the rocks, the sand, the water...

The first child disappeared on the last day of September that year, a bright faced boy of eight who left no more legacy than a sea soaked mitten and a scattering of press notices. Innocent eyes peered out from police posters in a bittersweet festive snapshot from the Christmas before. He was whisked away, according to the statements of his parents, from beneath their noses as they walked the sands. Nothing more was ever found of the child, his body assumed lost to the fickle pull of the tide, his parents absolved of blame in the absence of evidence to the contrary and the very palpable reality of their grief (unable to cope, his mother would take a long walk into the water some two years later leaving a neatly folded pile of clothes and a husband barely able to talk unless ordering his next drink). The loss was filed as accidental and nothing more was thought of it until, four weeks later, it happened again... and again... and again... over just three days four children were lost, two were strangers, the unfortunate offspring of two weekending families, the others were twin girls who had been born nine years earlier within earshot of the waves that had seemingly consumed them.

Like all communities the loss from within was felt more keenly than the loss from without. These were children that many had known by sight, by the sound of their voices as they had played outside the gift shop business their father had run on the promenade. There was no denying the actuality of their existence, the concrete *physicality* of it, and, with that acceptance, there was no denying the *loss* either. Tears were shed openly, flowers and messages placed carefully at the doorway of the shop (which would never again open its doors under the current owners; finding the sight of the water only feet from their welcome mat too much to deal with, they sold up and moved inland where last word has them making a go of things in a general store in the Lake District).

Then the foot was washed up on the sand.

Small and ragged, savaged by marine life, it was discovered by one time mayor of the town, Arnold Newman, while walking Smithers, his Yorkshire terrier.

He reportedly fainted when his ailing eyesight registered the object clamped in his dog's jaws as something altogether grislier than the tatty but much loved tennis ball he usually retrieved.

It was never conclusively agreed by the pathologists and their teams which of the missing children the foot had belonged to, but its existence begged the lie of an accidental verdict and the police resumed their investigation.

But they were, of course, looking in the wrong direction; the problem was in the water, as was, *again*, obvious to anyone with the sufficient instinct but to look.

But no one seemed to possess that instinct.

Until, that is, the Magician came to town.

ONE

This town would kill me one day...

... or so it seemed back then, caged by adverse geography and limited prospects.

I was at that awkward age, beyond child but long way from adult. The bleak coastline, the tawdry shops and arcades, the tatty carnival rides, they'd all lost their power to excite me (when once they had been the be all and end all of my existence). I didn't know what *would* excite me, and wouldn't for some time, caught by that wave of apathy that comes at the start of your teens. Give me a couple of years and new desires would kick in, music would mean passion and a girl's breasts would be something to fantasise about rather than giggle over. But for now escape was the thing, the almost compulsive need to be elsewhere and when, to be *other*.

Rare was the time that I was to be found outside the pages of a garish paperback, desperate to subsume my boring reality with something a little more vital and exciting, more *real*.

My parents ran a beach goods store, a fading shop-front filled with inflatable fancies and endless variations on the bucket (small ones large ones plain ones and castles) and the spade (from thin and flimsy to red steel deluxe). Racks of postcards, banal or bawdy, and sundry 'fancy' goods and rock filled the gaps. There was even a 'lovely line in shell' that my father could be heard to wax upon, various animals and monuments created prosaically from gluing shells of varying shapes and sizes together. Aside from the occasional convincing tortoise they were all atrocious bastardisations, fooling nobody.

Needless to say, it was a place I rarely loitered and my parents, after becoming aware of what a morose teenager slumped behind the till can do for trade, tended to allow my absence.

That year was an exception. After the disappearances of the children my free rein was severely curtailed. I was tied to either the house or the business, forbidden to wander alone outside the two. I complained of course, driven wild by my imprisonment. Not that it did any good, they were immovable, utterly convinced that I would be easy prey the minute I strayed from their sight.

Which shows what they knew.

I, of course, was equally convinced of my own invulnerability.

Which rather goes to show what *I* knew as well.

It would be wrong to pretend that I was unaffected by the atrocities that year, but it wasn't until the discovery of the foot that they really sunk in. Despite consuming words as reality with such gusto the news reports had had little effect, seeming distant and irrelevant. I had known the Masefield twins of course, their shop was only a short walk from ours and, while the slight age difference had put distance between us, we were far from strangers. Nonetheless it took the actual flesh to bring home to me that they were likely dead (and that something awful had happened to make them that way).

I actually caught a glimpse of the foot, having been at the shop that day to help my father unpack a delivery of traditional fudge selection packs that he hoped would help see us through the lean winter, 'ideal Christmas presents for anyone of discernment' he announced when pressed.

We'd heard Arthur Newman's cry when he clapped eyes on the body part but both of us had barely reacted; my father most likely assuming, as I did, that someone had been splashed by a stray wave or lost a hat to the strong wind that had been blowing that day. It was only when we heard the general noise of panic and saw people rushing past the doorway that we knew something was up.

The police were quick to arrive, Jeffery Collins, a constable in the town, had been loitering around the pier entrance (his soft spot for Julia Timmins in the ticket booth was as well known as her predilection for men in uniform) and had dashed onto the sands when hearing the noise. Once the sight of Arthur Newman pole-axed in a pile of seaweed and Smithers the terrier wagging his tail at the tasty find had sunk in he had shouted to Doug at the ice cream kiosk to lock up and get on the blower to headquarters. There must have been steel in his voice as Doug (a contrary gent at the best of times) had been straight out of the kiosk and jogging for a phone box at a speed not seen since a teenager had done a runner with a Ninety-Nine the season before.

By the time we got there Jeremy was keeping everyone back and uniforms were arriving in quantity. Nobody had any real idea what was going on, Arthur Newman had been pulled out of harm's way but had yet to really come round. Someone suggested that Smithers had gone mad and attacked his owner, noting how one of the other constables appeared to be struggling to restrain the small dog. The gathered crowd met this suggestion with considerable laughter; the notion of the tiny beast being a danger was more than most could swallow. No one thought much of Jeremy's uniform jacket lying on the sand until it was bundled up by Tony Reilly (first aid officer on the pier and closest we had to a medical authority in an emergency) and carried with some degree of panic towards a squad car.

In his haste he had fumbled the bundle slightly and the foot was visible on one side. It was Mary Watson, waitress in the café a few doors along from our shop who first recognised it for what it was, screaming at the limit of her lungs and pointing with one of her viciously long and crimson nails. It took a vigorous slap from Sandra Duckworth (trading name: Rosa Carlotta – 'All futures predicted, romantic entanglements a speciality') to bring her to her senses, the 'mystic' betraying her Northern roots with a whispered curse in a heavy Yorkshire accent before scrabbling in her sack of runes for a packet of Rothmans and a match.

Despite his inexperience and panic, Tony was quick to cover it up properly and get the package out of sight in his squad car.

It was too late for discretion however, those that hadn't *seen* had most certainly *heard* and the laughter and jollity ceased. For my part I can only admit to a strange feeling of calm, as if my brain had just accepted the facts, found them all to tally and then gently switched off. The foot had had a waxen quality, tatty, frayed and pale.

It looked so cold.

Due to its condition, the lack of identifiers and the bloat of salt water, I believe the foot was never apportioned an owner. Yet, in its own way, it belonged to the whole town that year; as absurd and macabre as that may sound, it took a small community and changed it for a while. It was a rare day that it wasn't heard mentioned somewhere amongst the shop queues, pub bars or across the back garden fences.

-1.2-

"The Devil's picture book tells many tales...

...comic, tragic, informative and foolish; the only certainty is uncertainty, the only guarantee is that there are... no... guarantees."

With that the Magician twisted his wrist and, seemingly from nowhere, it was filled with a pack of cards. There was a polite murmur of appreciation from the few people gathered but the wind was harsh and cold across the promenade and they were going to need greater miracles than that to keep them interested.

His appearance didn't help, appearing more like a down and out than a showman. Mid-thirties maybe, scruffy short hair, face unshaven. Instead of the prerequisite dinner jacket and bow tie he wore an open collar shirt, strangely cut black trousers and a large brown leather greatcoat that had a military look to it. To top it all off he was covered in jewellery, necklaces and bangles, crystals and beads – he was a few years early for the hippy movement and looked freakish to most eyes. There was no doubting his abilities however, hands and fingers blurred with a speed and precision I've never seen the like of again. He moved through a number of sleights and lifts that are familiar now but were invisible to me then. He warmed up with a run of basic forces, revealing the Queen of Hearts over and over again, peeling it off, slapping it down, tearing it up, peeling it off again. However he appeared to remove the Queen from the deck it would always reappear right back on the top. This garnered a little more appreciation; one lady even clapped her hands a few times.

Having got their attention he proceeded to shuffle and re-shuffle the deck in his left hand as, with the same flick of the wrist as before, another deck appeared in the right. He brought the two together, riffled and cut a few times, flipped them over to show the cards were varied and then placed them in a tiny stack on the portable table in front of him.

"They say that the key to a great story is the inability to see the end coming, while that may be true I like to buck the odds a little, plan ahead. For example, name a card, madam..."

He gestured to the lady that had clapped her hands. She blushed a little and mumbled the Eight of Clubs. The Magician smiled faintly, cut the deck, peeled off the card he'd cut to and revealed it on the table as the Eight. They all applauded a little at that, the woman stifled an embarrassed giggle with her hand and glanced at her friend as if for reassurance.

"A lucky guess, surely..." the Magician announced. "Perhaps someone else better try."

A large man pulled his wife closer to him, almost protectively, then suggested the Four of Diamonds. The Magician shrugged, cut the deck and, without looking himself, displayed the correct card to his gathered audience with an arcing of his hand. The applause was palpable now. Two young girls who I recognised from a few years above me at school dashed forward shouting a card each: Queen of Spades and Ten of Hearts. The Magician looked put out, as if them both shouting at once was a disturbance, then without even looking at the deck, he swept both hands through the cards and pulled the ones they had asked for, displaying one in each hand.

I pushed closer, determined to try my luck. Before I opened my mouth he looked straight at me, *into* me. Silently, and without looking away, he clicked his fingers and showed me the Jack of Clubs, the card that I had been thinking of. His stare broke and with a faint smile he shuffled the cards again, returning to his audience.

Later, after his show had finished and he was left to count his coins and put away his few props, I watched him from the safe distance of the shop doorway, a hundred yards or so away from his pitch.

The wind had picked up now, the Union Jack that hung from the mouth of the pier was whipping and cracking violently like snapping wood. The few visitors that had stumbled onto the front had dashed to the comfort of the indoor amusement arcades.

Once he had collected his things and flattened the table down to what looked like an impossibly thin suitcase, carried by its leather handle, he stood for a while, gazing out to sea. From within his coat pocket he removed a gunmetal cigar case and slid a Cuban into his palm. He put the case back and snipped the end of the cigar with a cutter from another pocket. Placing the cigar in his mouth he looked out to sea again, his face slightly troubled, like a man who thinks he hears his name being called only to find there's no one about him. The wind whipped at his leather coat, making the same noise as the flag only deeper, thicker.

He pulled out a box of matches, removed one, struck it on the sandpaper and held the flame steady to the end of his cigar. The flame burned, untouched by the wind, as calm as if within a room. He pulled and puffed a cloud of smoke into the air. It hung there, static, like a rain cloud seen from the ground. He turned and looked right at me, smiling. He put a black Fedora on his head, doffed it momentarily in my direction, then turned about and walked away along the promenade.

The cloud of smoke shifted and then dissipated, but before it vanished altogether I could have sworn it formed the shape of the suit of Clubs.

-1.3-

Dinnertimes were near fatal...

...in our house. There was something unquestionably lethal about gathering four people of mixed age and emotion around a table, grinding them together and then putting cutlery in their hands. To this day I'm surprised there were no casualties.

I don't know what it was about us but we just didn't *fit*. It was as if four utterly disparate people had been brainwashed and thrown together to live like a family, by evil scientists probably... all wild hair and steaming test tubes.

First there was Father, a man more suited to woollens than sheep themselves. When not pouring through catalogues full of shop products and getting unfeasibly excited about such tosh as inflatable globes or leatherette cigarette packet covers, he was heavily into steam engines. He could often be found tinkering with his own creation, *Silly Brigitte* (don't ask me, the name clearly meant something to Father but he never saw fit to enlighten us - and we didn't want to encourage him on his subject by asking), adjusting and experimenting, occasionally ducking from gusts of steam. It was that steam that gave him the unruly forelock of hair that sat perpetually erect on his scalp (or so we convinced ourselves when out of his earshot). Having allegedly pursued a career in engineering from an early age it had been meeting our mother (a common euphemism for 'getting her pregnant') that had scotched his plans and forced him to seek alternative forms of breadwinning. How he made the sudden leap to beach goods was beyond us (and, truth be told, a big enough cause for suspicion when hearing his tales of a misspent youth with pressure pumps).

But, if he was rather exaggerative about the past then his wife was no better. An outrageous glamour puss who, in her cups, seemed held together by no more than a thick covering of pancake and enough lip gloss to weatherproof the shed where Father stored *Silly Brigitte*. Full of tales about her formative years in the theatre, and the perpetual narrow scrapes with the West End and Hollywood (she would have been the next Rita Hayworth if it hadn't been for a broken high heel and a missed bus ride – or so the epic saga of the 'movie audition' went – an old favourite often brought out and dusted down at social functions). Once her pregnancy with Jeremy put a stop to her high-kicking ways she settled down to a quiet life of bitterness and gentle resentment broken up by part time shifts at the *Vegas Slots* amusement arcade, which kept her in Dunhills and Vodka on a Friday night. She eventually left Dad for a shoe salesman from Colchester, I'm not sure he's noticed yet.

Jeremy was my elder brother, a lanky creature who had ambitions of being a Mod for most of his teenage years. He threatened to leave us weekly, just as soon as he got the crippled Vespa he'd bought for a slight fold of paper from a passing fairground carnie roadworthy. He formed a band called *The Fat Zero* which assaulted local pub audiences with warmed over Who covers for a few years before disbanding by popular demand. He never did get that Vespa on the road and now earns a living working for a company in Southampton that manufacture flat-pack kitchen units.

And then there was me...

Which just goes to show: genetics aren't always reliable.

I mentioned the Magician at the dinner table for the sake of safe small talk. Forgetting of course my Mother's seemingly infinite past.

"Gypsies, tramps and thieves, Gregory, the lot of them," she offered, while trying to thrash some life into a pork chop that was beginning to set in the pool of gravy on her plate. "I worked as an assistant to the Great Zardozi for a season in Blackpool once, spent most nights keeping him off the bottle 'til he went on stage, then avoiding the attention of his 'magic wand' once he got off it. He was a bigger threat to rabbits than myxamatosis, caused many a tear at children's parties. He broke his neck falling into an orchestra pit in Rhyll in the end; biggest applause he ever got."

With this she gave up on her meal and got up from the table for a smoke. Ladies and gentlemen, Fenella Ashe has left the building.

"I quite like magicians," Dad offered, chewing on his pork chop. He stared into space for a while, whether contemplating illusions or overcooked pig I couldn't tell. This was quite common; easily distracted by some momentary thought or feeling, conversations with him could often be like verbal archaeology. "Very skilled people," he eventually concluded, rather anti-dramatically, returning to his dinner.

Jeremy lived up to expectations by grunting, shoving his plate out of the way and striding out of the kitchen as if deeply insulted by the very air we all breathed. It must have been difficult being an angry young man full time; I occasionally caught him fighting to stifle a good mood. We all had our cross to bear, I suppose.

***

I dreamed I was back on the front. The sea was rough and stormy, hurling flotsam and jetsam of body parts and children's toys onto the sand. I picked my way through them, pausing to notice the little head of Jessica Masefield wearing a thick spray of seaweed as if it were a wig, her eyes cool and shining like marbles. As I watched, a small crustacean scurried out of the slimy fronds and across her face. I cried a few tears for her, salt-water sympathy, and then moved on towards the pier, a fossilised spine emerging from the ground, rusted iron scar.

In the web of girders and struts beneath the pier the Magician was sat at his fold-out table playing cards with the clown automaton from the pier entrance. He riffled and cut the pack before dealing a pair of poker hands. They played for a while, the Magician puffing on a cigar, the clown moving stiffly as it reached for its cards, the white makeup on its fingers and face cracking like dry plaster with every movement. Beneath its satin suit there was a constant castanet chatter, small bulges and waves rippling in the soft material from something shifting in its innards.

The gambling began. Small spheres, like those in the vending machines on the promenade, were thrown in a pile. These were not filled with disposable rain hats or plastic jewellery, however, something liquid splashed in their bellies, pushing against the inside, trying to get out

The clown played a straight; the Magician chuckled and splayed the Royal Family of Hearts on the table.

"You weren't born to bluff, my friend." The Magician spoke around his cigar. "Not with that face." He pulled the spheres to his side of the table but the clown's hand shot out and grabbed his wrist, a small puff of white powder erupting from its knuckles. One of the spheres rolled off the table and fell to the ground where it cracked open on a pebble. The air was filled with the sound of a baby's cry and the sharp smell of salt water, fading as the silvery liquid seeped away into the sand.

"Double or quits?" the Magician asked. Slowly the clown extended its other hand and pointed directly at me. "Don't trust me, huh?" the Magician chuckled. "Can't think why." With a click of his fingers he produced an Ace from behind the clown's ear. The Magician turned towards me, half of his face obscured by cigar smoke, like a moon draped in cloud. "Come closer, kid."

Behind me the sea roared, and underneath the sound of the waves I could have sworn I heard Jessica Masefield crying.

I stepped up to the table.

"What do you want me to do?" I asked. The Magician gathered the cards and placed them in a neat stack in the centre of the table.

"Cut the cards," he said, leaning back. I extended my hand slowly but fell short of the pack, scared to touch them. "Go on kid," he said. "Cut 'em, they won't bleed."

When I touched the pack I felt a small static tingle and the sound of Jessica's tears grew louder behind me.

"For you," the Magician said, pointing towards the clown, who nodded slowly and looked at me, its cracking grin smeared like a bloodstain, stretching even wider.

I showed the card I had cut to: the Ten of Spades. The clicking from inside the clown grew louder; white noise.

"Now me," said the Magician as I put the cards back. He looked right at me as he had done on the promenade earlier. That fierce stare that seemed to penetrate beyond the flesh, the stare that had known the card I had in my head before I could even say its name out loud.

I cut the deck to reveal, of course, the Jack of Clubs. The Magician winked at me and passed his hands over the table making all the spheres, his and the clown's, disappear. The clown turned to me, laughing that terrible tin row it performed at the press of a button, its wound of a mouth stretching wider and wider and wider, the clicking from its belly growing louder, drowning out the humourless laugh. Most of its face was now a black hole lined with grey and yellow teeth, the rest of its features crumpled and distorted around it. From within the darkness emerged the source of the clicking; crabs pulled themselves free of its guts, snapping their pincers violently. They flowed over what was left of its face and shoulders. There was an almighty crack as its satin suit erupted in many simultaneous holes, more creatures appearing from within it. Faintly I was aware of the Magician shouting at me to get back. I didn't need his advice, as I stumbled away from the table, distancing myself from this monstrosity.

But I had moved in the wrong direction, as I turned to run a colossal wave towered above me and, achieving form, swallowed me whole.

-1.4 -

That was my first sticky sheet experience...

...and, aside from a bizarre dream concerning a field of breasts that occurred a year or so later (disturbing to me at the time – hilarious now) it would also be my last. I was coated in sweat, the bedding wrapped around me tighter than a noose.

I bundled the wet sheets together and threw them in the washing machine (in that foolish child logic that suggests this will be less suspicious than simply leaving them there) and, after a long bath, headed to the beach.

It was still early, the promenade quiet and the cafés empty. I decided to blag myself a milkshake from Rita and waste a few hours with a book. Sandra Duckworth was at one of the tables, cleaning some muck out of her nails with a tarot card and smoking up a fury as usual. I sat opposite her, my banana milkshake making me feel as American as Kennedy.

"Do me a reading," I asked with the same tone that had won me the milkshake.

"Don't be a bugger, love, I've got a migraine on me that could cripple an elephant."

This was typical, classic Duckworth if you will. For a woman who plied her trade in mystical trappings she had all the charm and magic of a Doc Marten boot.

I sipped at my milkshake for a bit, flicking through the paperback (a battered Lovecraft, or possibly Ray Bradbury, I can't remember), waiting for this silent drip-effect to achieve critical mass. She must have had a really rough night because it was only a few minutes before she slapped the card on the Formica and fixed me with a stare.

"You're a royal pain in the arse, you know that?" she hissed.

"But charming with it," I grinned. "What do you think about dreams?"

"Not much." She sighed, gazing out of the window at the lazy autumn sea. "Although, God help us, we'd be lost without them." She looked sad for a moment, lost even, before her cynical mask dropped back into place. "Why, you been wetting the bed?"

I flustered for a moment, embarrassed at how unintentionally close she was.

"Of course not, just wondering, that's all."

"Hmm, whatever you say." She sipped at her coffee, scowled at its coldness and lit another cigarette. "Nightmares is it?" she mouthed through a cloud of smoke. I nodded, before it even occurred to me to lie.

Outside the window I saw Mary Watson walking along the promenade towards us, ready to start her waitressing shift. She glanced out towards the sea and suddenly stopped. Her face fell slack and her handbag dropped from her hand spilling its contents all over the floor. She was staring towards the beach by the pier.

"Oh Christ," muttered Sandra, getting to her feet, "what now?"

Mary screamed and raised her hand to her mouth as if to force the cry back in. Others had noticed her now and had started to look in the same direction. Sandra ran out of the café and I followed quickly.

Outside a small crowd had begun to gather, all staring at the sand. Standing just beyond the ebbing tide was a small girl, naked and shivering in the cold breeze. For a second I couldn't understand why everyone was just staring, then I realised who it was, she looked so unrecognisable, her hair matted into thick strands standing out from her reddened face. Jessica Masefield.

"Don't just stand there!" came a shout from behind. "Someone fetch help." The Magician pushed past me and jumped down onto the sand, running towards the girl and pulling his coat from his shoulders. His voice broke the moment and someone ran to fetch Tony Reilly and his first aid box, someone else must have rung the police because they arrived a few minutes later.

The Magician gathered Jessica in his coat, swamping her in the leather, and bundled her into his arms. Carefully, he carried her back to the promenade.

Someone must have called her father because he came sprinting from up the road and, stumbling off the promenade into the sand, snatched his daughter and held her tight, dropping to his knees and sobbing her name over and over. It terrified me to see a big man reduced to such a wreck, face wet from snot and tears, mumbling incoherently as he stroked his daughter's hair. Someone tried to help him up but he pushed them away and, licking his fingers, started to try and wipe the muck from her face.

The Magician walked away calmly, the ever-present cigar appearing, already lit, in his fingers. I doubt anyone else noticed this small impossibility, attentions all fixed on the reunited father and child, but after my dream the night before, I watched the man's every movement, searching for miracles.

He appeared utterly separate from the rest of us. Most people were anxious, some had joined the father in his tears, the rest all talked at once, asking questions or making up answers. He just stood to one side, puffing away. After a moment I realised that he wasn't looking at the girl or her father. He seemed more interested in the beach, scrutinising the sand and the shadows beneath the pier. After a moment he walked in that direction and, unsure of quite why, I found myself following.

I caught up with him under the pier, he was on his haunches, prodding at the great mounds of seaweed that always gathered there like discarded fishing nets. He didn't look up as I drew closer, but he must have noticed me as he began to speak.

"The key to solving any magic trick is to look first at what is utterly impossible and then work backwards."

"'When you have excluded the impossible, whatever remains, however improbable, must be the truth'" I muttered.

He did look up then, smiling.

"Well read, I see. Tell me then, 'Holmes', what would you make from the facts in hand?"

I looked around but the point escaped me.

"I don't know what you mean."

"The seaweed here is undisturbed." He got to his feet and gently popped some of its air sacs with the toe of his boot. "The beach in the other direction is completely open and anyone walking from that direction would have to pass Bill Clements putting out his deck chairs, not to mention the lifeboat shed where I see that Joe Rigby has been waterproofing the boat for most of the morning." He took another puff on his cigar. "So where did she appear from?"

I looked around, slowly grasping his point. If Jessica had walked along the beach from any angle she would surely have been seen long before she was.

"I don't know, it's impossible"

"Improbable you mean. There really is only one other direction." We walked out from under the pier and he looked out to sea.

"The water you mean?"

"Elementary."

"But that's..."

"Disturbing." He watched the waves for a moment before turning back to me, a smile on his face. "I fancy a coffee, come on, I'll buy you a milkshake." He walked back up the beach towards the promenade. I paused for a moment, wary of this strange man. He stopped, turned around and sighed, then stared at me deeply.

"*Trust me.*"

And I did, following him obediently up the beach.

"I'd better try and get my coat back as well, ferret in the wrong pocket and the poor girl will be swamped with doves."

Like an embolism in leather...

...brain fever. Haemorrhage. There was something about him, a power that was physically felt. The headache that loiters under a double dose of Ibuprofen, painless yet tender, an awareness of something amiss within the grey matter. Was it something like gravity? The presence of a greater mind affecting lesser minds within its presence? Mental tides?

I don't know what I had expected, some form of explanation, some form of plan. I certainly hadn't expected him to fill a table at the café with a house of cards in the style of a Venetian palace. Apparently it helped him concentrate. As did the coffee, which he drank endlessly, draining each cup in a matter of a couple of mouthfuls.

After half an hour or so I felt I should push him as to answers; where were the children being taken? What was taking them? Why? Why? Why?

"Elsewhere, something, answers on a postcard..." he muttered hunting in the sugar bowl for a few lumps of brown.

"Why won't you tell me?" I shouted, banging the Formica and taking out the east wing of the Doge's Palace. With a yell he stuck out a hand to support the rest of the cards, which somehow it did, the entire lattice resting gently on a fingertip while he put the fallen cards back one-handed.

"It's not that I won't tell you, it's that I don't know... that and the lack of practical words. Listen, you're suddenly becoming aware that there's more to existence than the reality you were previously aware of, it's difficult, confusing, but so is trying to explain it." Sighing, he went to drink more coffee before realising he couldn't move without destroying the card construction. He gave a faint growl and carried on building.

"Tell me, what do you want out of life?" he asked, while he built.

"I don't know, money... happiness."

"That doesn't answer my question; money is a means to something else, not a goal in itself, happiness is the ultimate effect. *What* do you want? Are you happy with what you've already got?"

"No..."

"So you want more, more than what?"

"More than this?"

"That's what's out there, indefinable, indescribable, but most certainly more than *this*." He gestured vaguely with his head then noticed my book. "Imagine a book worm, working its way through the pages of a Full English Dictionary that sits on a shelf surrounded by thousands of other books; in a library, in a street, in a city, in a country, in a world, in a galaxy, in a universe. Ask that worm to describe the rest of the wall its shelf sits on and its brain would struggle to conceive of it, so how could it describe the universe? Do you begin to understand how difficult it might be to casually explain what lies beyond that existence? That's why your species invented gods, makes the whole thing much easier."

"*Your* species?"

"Hmm, the less said about them the better, we'll be here all day." With that he finished replacing the cards and drained his coffee. "Fancy another milkshake?"

"Not really. So you're saying that they were taken by something we don't know from outside of reality for reasons best known to itself?"

"In a nutshell. *Probably.* "

"But that's... awful."

"Obviously, I wouldn't be suggesting we put a stop to it otherwise, would I? You're sure you don't want another milkshake? Slice of cake?"

"No."

"Fair enough...I might get another coffee." He waved at Rita who nodded and turned to the coffee maker. "Maybe even a slice of lemon cake, it's important to keep the blood sugar up if you're planning on battling pan-dimensional entities."

Sandra came in, the gust of wind from the door wiping out the card palace.

"Oh well," he said in a flutter of cards. "It was bound to happen eventually."

Sandra walked over.

"Alright Gregory," she said, eyeing the Magician with

suspicion. "And you are...?"

"Unusual. Fancy a coffee?" I noticed that look in his eyes again, the one that worked its way into your head.

"Don't mind if I do, budge up young man." She pushed in next to me, patting me on the thigh as she did so. I must have pulled some kind of face because the Magician chuckled and winked at me.

"I've seen you working the crowds on the front, very good I hear."

"Thank you."

"Are you just passing through, Mister...?"

"Dallion, and no, looks like I'll be staying, if I can find a bed for a few weeks."

"Dallion? What sort of name is that?"

"About as likely as Rosa Carlotta...'Sandra'."

"Hmm, point taken, do you smoke?"

"Furiously, thank you." He took one of her offered cigarettes and lit it from a flame on his index finger.

"Bloody show off." She took his hand and lit her cigarette off it, not one to be thrown.

"Saves losing lighters all the time."

She smiled and I became aware of something going on between them.

"If you're pushed for somewhere to stay I've a spare room that's sitting empty, chip in with the bills and I'm sure we can come to some sort of arrangement.

"That would be wonderful, thank you."

Simple as that.

Rita brought the coffees over and Dallion put a pound note into her hand, cheering her up no end.

"Well, I better get on, gather up some things... stuff... what have you. I'll see you at the house later if that's alright?"

"Fine."

"Right then." He winked at me, and got to his feet. "I'll see you tomorrow, I'm sure."

"Don't you want your coffee?" I asked.

"Ah..." He picked up the mug and put it in his coat pocket. "I'll have it later. Tell Rita not to worry, I'll bring the mug back."

It was only after he'd left that Sandra realised she hadn't told him where she lived.

"Something tells me he'll find it," I reassured her.

TWO

Number 33 stays up late, whether she wants to or not.

The sound of number 35's prayers and supplications (as the risen Jesus, number 35 was a dedicated evangelist) and the sobbing of 38 as she tried to remember her son's name, would go on way after lockdown. There are some in here, she knows, who blanket out the sounds of the other 'patients' by focusing on the sound of the waves. Concentrate hard on the sound of the water biting at the rock face below until they hear nothing else, rocked to sleep.

Number 33 prefers the sobbing.

The sea is inside her head; her brain tastes of salt. Even beyond the cranial enema of pharmaceuticals they keep her full of - her guts rattle with lithium - she can taste the water, harsh at the back of her throat, burning like the onset of a head cold. The last thing, the *very* last thing, she wants is to think about it.

Let 35 pray, let 38 bawl, there's nothing in either that can hurt her.

Not that they'll stop any time soon, especially tonight, when the moon is full and pouring its grey light into each and every room. Tonight there's a chorus from the damned, even the quieter inmates are feeling the need to make themselves heard. Earlier, number 46 had thrown herself against the wall of her cell in an attempt to escape. Repeatedly. Running at full strength towards the brick, colliding, sliding to the floor, crawling back and then running again. First the sound was nothing but a dull thud and a grunt but after twenty or so attempts it began to dampen, number 46 sobbing as she lost skin to the bricks. Number 33 thought the popping sound had probably been her arm dislocating, pulled from its socket like a drumstick. The warders stopped her eventually, pulled her from her room and dragged her screaming to the infirmary.

Number 29 made promises she was in no position to keep, offering the moon her heart, her soul, her sex. She offered everything if it would only take her. Take her away from all this.

The moon made no reply.

It wasn't that number 33 didn't feel the lunar pull, the tightening of hair follicles, the static charge. She felt it stronger than most of them, knew it intimately. She also knew what it was the moon wanted, knew that number 29 didn't have a chance of giving it. Number 29 was too old. The moon liked them young. Fresh. Number 33 knew this from experience, and if only they would listen to her she knew what it would take to make it stop.

But who listens to the insane?

-2.2-

Lisa wants Jeremy's babies.

That's what it had said. Carved with a compass needle into the soft wood of the desk lid then highlighted in ink. Maybe that's all it had taken. All that had been needed to make him run a mile, to tell her to get lost in front of everyone she knew: her friends, her class, the rest of the band. All of them, laughing or looking away in embarrassment, watching as she made a fool of herself with the waterworks, as she dropped the bottle stolen from her parent's drinks cabinet, as she stared at the broken glass and damp patches of gin on the toes of her cheap damn shoes, as she turned tail and ran out of the hall. Maybe that's what it had been.

She hadn't even been the one that wrote it.

The promenade was cold, the wind blowing off the sea making her freckled arms blister into goose flesh, her sand coloured hair blowing apart from its hair spray styling, the 'look' she had laboured over for as long as it took to make it appear that she hadn't laboured over it at all.

It was quiet out here, too cold for anyone with their heart still intact. Half an hour ago someone had stumbled out of The Anchor and thrown up on the beach, emptied his guts onto the sand and broken shells for a couple of minutes, wiped his mouth, relieved himself and then, laughing if you please, jogged back inside to fill back up. She'd shrunk back on her bench, letting the shadows hide her, and waited until he'd gone. Since then she'd been alone.

Just her and the waves.

So where had the man come from? He was stood a couple of hundred yards away along the promenade. Stock still, silhouetted by the streetlights on the road. She got up and began to walk in the opposite direction, towards the pier and the main road, the lights and The Anchor. The pub was kicking out, a few men stumbling onto the pavement. She tried to recognise the one who had been sick earlier but she hadn't got a good look at him and couldn't tell if he was among them or not. Glancing over her shoulder she noticed that the man was following, not rushing but clearly heading towards her. She dashed onto the road in a panic, running headlong into a drunk and sending him to the floor.

"Watch where you're running, you silly cow!" he slurred, getting to his feet. Then he smiled, *badly*, and came close to her. She squirmed as he put his hand on her arm, wrinkling her nose at the smell of cheap beer and filterless cigarettes. "You all on your own darlin'?" he asked, pushing even closer to her. She tried to move away but he grabbed her other arm and pulled her into a forced hug.

"She's with me," said a voice behind her. The drunk let her go and she turned to look at the man who had been stood on the promenade. His face seemed vaguely familiar, messy blond hair and long leather coat.

"Really?" chuckled the drunk. "You're twice her age; should be bloody ashamed of yourself." With that he stumbled off, swearing under his breath.

Lisa hugged herself, suddenly aware of the cold. The stranger sat on the promenade wall and reached into his pocket, retrieving a cigar, before ferreting in his pocket again and pulling something else out which he held out towards her.

"Keep out the cold," he explained, lighting his cigar. It appeared to be a mug of tea or coffee, gently steaming in the cold air. "Are you alright?"

"Yes." Then, after a moment's thought, "Thank you."

"Don't worry about it. Drink your coffee."

Without really thinking she took it and drank a mouthful, it was intensely sweet.

"Better?"

"Much."

"Good, it's a bit late to be hanging around down here, you know. I think you should finish your drink and get off home. Your parents are worried about you."

She drained the mug, shivering slightly at the sugariness of it.

"I suppose so." Then something occurred to her. "How can you carry a mug of coffee in your coat without spilling it?"

"Magic!" he said, making a playing card appear from thin air and pressing it into her hand. "Besides, not spilling it is easy, keeping it hot, that's the tricky part. Now, go home."

"Sorry." She handed him back the mug and he put it in his pocket and walked off up the road.

"Thank you!" she called, watching him go for a minute before turning round and heading off towards the pier. She tried to look at the card in her hand but it was too dark. Glancing around she saw the automaton clown's booth was lit and walked up to it so that she could see clearly. It was the Queen of Hearts.

Which made her feel much better somehow.

The clown's hand shot through the thick glass of the booth and clamped her tightly by the face, its mildew-scented glove stopping the scream of surprise in her throat. She kicked out as it stepped down from its gold-paint throne and onto the path next to her but her foot connected with dead wood and had no effect as it grabbed her hair and pulled her towards the sand.

The Queen of Hearts fell to the ground, landing face up in the broken glass as the clown pulled her slowly into the shadows under the pier.

Forced back onto a bed of seaweed Lisa began to cry helplessly as the automaton chuckled its tin laugh and lowered its chattering mouth towards her, it's stiff and unnatural body holding her down.

She still hoped for help as she passed out, waited for the strange man to save her again even as the clown began to feed.

It took the eyes first.

-2.3-

Number 33 felt like laughing...

...and God help her, she had no idea why.

THREE

The air was cancerous...

...thick with curtains of cigar smoke both fresh and aging that hung in the occasional sunlight like oil in water. Beneath the stench of it all was the scent of coffee and whisky. Chaos everywhere, perhaps the room had taken a sincere look at its occupant and shuffled into synchronicity. Bedding writhed on the floor like discarded funeral shrouds, chairs overturned, books piled in heaps where they had thrown themselves suicidally from the shelves above them. It was dark, lit only by the beams of daylight that fell through the gaps of ill-fitting curtains.

"She's only let you in because she thinks you'll get me to talk," said a voice in the corner.

"Which proves she cares," I replied.

"It proves how bloody irritating she is, you sanctimonious sod, you've a lot to learn about women."

"I've a lot to learn in general, stupidly I hoped you might teach me some of it."

Dallion leaned forward, his unshaven face catching in the light.

"Christ, kid, if I really knew anything worth knowing do you really think I'd be sat here? Now bugger off and make me a coffee. Lots of it."

***

After the murder of Lisa Thompson I saw nothing of the Magician for several days. I kept expecting to spot him in the mess of broken glass and nervous uniforms at the morning-after crime scene, hunting for stray cigar smoke out of the corner of my eye. Once or twice I had gone round to Sandra's house in the hope of speaking to one or the other. Despite repeated ringing of the doorbell no one came. Once I thought I caught a glimpse of someone between the drawn curtains of one of the upstairs windows but my shouts had only brought the attentions of Sandra's belligerent next-door neighbour who told me to 'sling my hook' in no uncertain terms.

It wasn't just the desperate need to talk to them about what had happened, I had something I needed to return to him. Something the wind, or perhaps the scuffle of the victim, had brushed into the dirt of the flowerbeds that circled the entrance to the pier.

The atmosphere at home was even more terse than usual, even the vague attempts at dinner conversation had faded away leaving us to chew our congealing mess in silence. Jeremy was particularly affected. I was pretty sure he had known Lisa and had asked him how he was doing, a rare moment of concern in our relationship. He shot me a distasteful look and told me to 'piss off'. I heard him crying in his room later that night and decided to drop it.

It was ten days before I had any luck. I'd gone to the house again, rung the bell a few times and then sat on the garden wall refusing to take no for an answer. When Sandra opened the door you could tell she had been crying, her eyes were puffy and rimmed with dark crescents. She gave me a half smile and beckoned me in.

"Where've you been?" I asked her. She looked at me sorrowfully and lit a cigarette.

"I haven't left the house for days." She looked at the pack of cigarettes she was holding rattled it and frowned, "Supplies are getting short."

She sighed and then, bizarrely, kissed me on the forehead and, grabbing her handbag, began to head out of the door.

"He's upstairs, good luck to you, love, I'll be back in a bit."

With that she strolled out of the house, leaving the door open behind her, and vanished off up the street.

***

On my return to his room, two mugs of coffee in my hands, my first impression was that he had left while my back was turned. Perhaps sent me to get him a drink so that he could dash out of the house while I was distracted. It was only when a pile of clothes in the corner stood up that I realised he had been in front of me all the time. He took one of the mugs off me, drained it and then, after looking for somewhere flat to put it down, gave it back to me, taking the full mug in exchange.

"Thanks, how much sugar?"

"Six in each."

"Good enough."

"Can I open a window?"

"If you must, just don't let too much light in."

I pulled one of the curtains halfway back and swung the window wide open, taking a deep lungful of fresh air, like a deep sea diver taking the opportunity to top up. I reached into my jacket pocket, took out the blood stained Queen of Hearts I had found and handed it to him.

"I found that by the pier, thought it was probably yours." I heard him sigh and place it in his pocket.

"Now you're hiding evidence for me."

"You didn't kill her."

"Really? What makes you so sure?"

"Because I trust you."

"Of course you do. Why do you think that is?"

It was a good question and, for the life of me I couldn't really answer it.

"I just do."

"You trust me, Gregory, because I told you too, nothing more. You don't even know me. Don't know the first thing about me; you don't even know my *name* for God's sake."

"Dallion."

"That's not my name, not my *real* name. It's just the first thing I say when I can't think of anything else."

"So what *is* your real name?"

"Why? Do think knowing it would make the difference?"

He took out a pack of cards and shuffled them one-handed. Then he started 'juggling'; popping one card out of the full deck into his empty hand and then tossing it back in to replace with another.

"What am I Gregory? A hero? A fool?"

He threw the whole pack in the air where it disappeared, leaving a solitary card on his palm: the card I had found by the pier, the Queen of Hearts.

"A Magician? A man who deprives you of your sensibilities for a fee? A charlatan... a *fake*? Is that someone truly deserving of your faith? I'm a manipulator; everything I say is intended to create a specific effect. How else do you think I managed to get a room to stay in from a total stranger within minutes of meeting her? How else would I convince a curious yet wary boy to offer me complete and utter trust? I manipulated both of you."

"And now you're trying to convince me that you're unworthy of my trust."

He smiled, it looked as alien as a moustache on a baby.

"You're a smartarse, Gregory."

There was silence, he folded the playing card away into his pocket and looked towards the light from the slightly parted curtains. I stared at his face, trying to understand him, trying to *know* him. I've said that he appeared to be in his mid-thirties, which was certainly true and yet, now, scrutinising his face, reading every line and flaw it seemed to miss the mark completely. It wasn't that he looked older in his features, the face was that of a man still looking forward to middle age; sufficient youth to remind you of what he might have been, sitting alongside the creases that predicted what he would become. But somewhere beyond the physical features there was a hint of something more. It was in the eyes certainly, a light brown turning to green that held more than his mouth would ever say. Beyond that though, it was something slightly inferred, a slipping mask that suggested more detail beneath.

"Did you kill her?" I asked, keeping my eyes on his face, watching for traces of a lie.

He turned his eyes directly to me and there seemed to be the beginnings of a tear in the left.

"I don't know."

This wasn't either of the answers I had expected; the question seemed fairly cut and dry to me, pretty black and white. Was he claiming some mental aberration, a plea of insanity from the bench?

"You mean you don't remember?"

This surprised him, confused him almost.

"Of course not, I mean that while I didn't touch her it

might have been my fault that she was touched. Maybe it was intended as a message, a threat even."

"So all this is just guilt?"

He thought for a moment.

"Yes, but not in the way that you mean. When I first heard that she'd been murdered my immediate thought was not of pity for her... It was of fear for me."

I let this thought hang for a moment, uncertain of how I felt. Was it so callous?

"You're only human," I said eventually. He looked at me then, the smile back on his face, more genuine than before.

"Which just goes to prove how little you know me."

-3.2 -

"He's mad as arseholes...

...you do realise that don't you?"

Sandra took a sip of her tea and the glasses she wore for reading clouded over in a haze of condensation. I could tell she wasn't herself because she didn't swear; she simply put the mug down on the small table by her armchair and wiped her glasses on her blouse with a sigh. In front of her there was a full spread of tarot cards.

"You're doing a reading?" I asked, frankly rather surprised.

"Don't be stupid, lad, the bloody corner shop was closed, I'm playing patience to take my mind off cigarettes."

"Oh."

"Of course, I can't possibly win because I lost the Six of Pentacles down the back of an amp at a Kinks' gig last year. Still, keeps me busy. You heard what I said?"

"Yes, but I don't think he's mad."

"Don't get me wrong, love, it doesn't bother me one jot."

She took another sip of her tea.

"I've always felt at home with people off the beaten mental track, says a lot about me I suppose.

"I remember when I was a kid my folks took me to

50

York for the day, it was like a foreign world to a lass from Huddersfield, everything was so bloody *nice*. The best bit was walking round the old city walls, not because I liked the walk, you had to keep getting on and off the damn things because of gaps, but because of a bloke I met there. He called himself a Lord; don't know if it was true, he certainly dressed like one; all tweed jacket, waistcoat and watch chain. He wasn't that old I suppose, middle aged. He told us he could see people's 'colours', insisted on drawing mine. It was just this swirl of red, green and purple on a cheap piece of sketch paper, but I loved it. He asked for money of course, to help maintain his estate he said. Father paid him, more to keep me happy then out of any notion of value, I'm sure. I spent the rest of the day wondering what it would be like to walk around seeing all these streaks of colour, great blazing ribbons hanging off everything. I suppose it could just have been a con, a way of making an easy buck, but I honestly don't think so, he had a lunatic sincerity about him, as well as a faint arrogance, as if it was a little demeaning for a peer of the realm to be buggering about among the hoi polloi with a fistful of crayons. Which I suppose it was. I can't help wondering what became of him, whether he kept on seeing colours among strangers or whether he ended up in a padded room. It's strange though how he seems more important to me now than my friends at school, more *real* somehow. Wish I hadn't lost the picture he drew for me.

"Then ten years later I met a man who said he could read your future from a few strands of your pubic hair..."

"Ugh! Could he?"

"Nope, but he had one hell of a collection."

We both laughed at that, thank God, the atmosphere lifting a hundredfold.

"*You're* definitely mad, Sandra."

"One hundred percent, satisfaction guaranteed, money back if not convinced, certifiable, darling."

"'Nobody here but us chickens...'" announced Dallion as he burst into the room making Sandra spill her tea in surprise.

"You silly bastard, you nearly gave me a heart

attack!"

He threw her a carton of Rothmans cigarettes.

"See if that helps."

Then he turned to me and pointed angrily, the spitting image of every schoolteacher I'd ever known.

"As for you, you reckless sod, if you're absolutely determined to tag along then you'll at least give me the satisfaction of freaking you out a bit more. Follow me."

-3.3 -

"I took a trip on a Gemini Starship…"

I assumed his lunatic singing and frantic thigh drumming was a sign of an uplifted mood, although it could equally have been proof undeniable of Sandra's 'Out of His Skull' theory.

We were back in his room upstairs. It was still frantically untidy but he had cleared a space on the floor where we sat facing each other.

"What are we going to do?" I asked, frankly rather worried.

"We're going on a mental stroll."

"Right. You couldn't explain that a bit better could you?"

He chuckled.

"It's actually very simple; throughout time people have practised the art of separating the mind from the body, un-anchoring oneself from the flesh and allowing the spirit to travel through so called 'higher-planes' free from all that irritating physics. There's nowhere you can't go, back in history or forward into potential future, stopping off at every possible dimension or imagined existence en route. It's wonderfully useful for intelligence gathering."

"But how can you separate the mind from the body?"

"Through a considered effort to dissolve one's grip on physical reality. Many have used psychedelic drugs to facilitate it but I wouldn't recommend that unless you're happy to travel to other dimensions laughing like a loon pointing at everything in the belief that it's the Tree of Life. It takes considerable experience to maintain one's control when your brain's frying on a dose sufficient to cause a hippo's bowels to prolapse. A seasoned traveller spends many years training himself to divorce himself mentally at the flip of a brain switch but we haven't time to mess about with that so may I suggest that you take several big mouthfuls of that and leave the driving to me."

He passed me a bottle of Bourbon whiskey.

"But... I'm not old enough to drink."

Alright, I admit that was a pretty redundant thing to say in the circumstances but I was out of my depth and my brain was farting nonsense whenever I opened my mouth.

"Just do it and try not to throw up all over my coat."

I grabbed the bottle and took a large mouthful, gagging at the harshness of it, my hand coming up to my mouth to stop me spitting it all over the carpet. It burned all the way down my throat, churning in my gut as it hit my stomach. To this day I struggle with whiskey, the basic chemical memory of my first drink being enough to put me off every time. I took another mouthful and found it a little easier having got over the initial shock.

"Put this on," he said, taking the bottle off me and handing me one of the necklaces he wore. It was a fat chunk of amber hanging from a silver chain.

"Do I have to?" I said weakly, biting down on the liquid-jaw instinct to be sick.

He just stared at me, sighing. I slipped the thing around my neck. "Why do you wear all of that stuff anyway? It looks silly."

He smiled. "Thank you for your fashion advice, I'll bear it in mind. Most of them have specific purposes actually, functional rather than aesthetic." He rattled a bangle on his wrist. "This opens a sealed tomb in Bangladesh. This one..." he held a long string of beads out from his chest "...has karmic properties."

"What about this one?" I asked, pointing to the unwieldy lump under my shirt.

"It sets off the green in my eyes! Enough questions."

He closed his eyes and drew in a long breath. "Right: out of neutral, slip it into first and off we go..."

The next thing I was aware of was a rushing of motion, a fizz of alcohol filtering into my brain and then the feel of sand beneath my feet. After a moment I realised my eyes were tightly closed so I opened them. All around me was a wasteland of black sand. Sharp, crystalline, like dyed sugar. There were great mountains of it all around us, and somewhere the vague scent of factory smoke. Dallion was walking a few feet ahead of me, which was rather disturbing as I still clearly felt his hand surrounding mine.

"I can still feel you," I called, jogging to catch up.

"Basic physical memory; you're experiencing two levels of reality and your mind is struggling to deal with both, you can still feel my hand because back there our bodies are sat in the room and I'm still holding it. Your mind, however, is out here with me and it knows that it should feel the sand beneath your feet and the wind in your hair because that is what it's seeing. They should resolve themselves in a minute."

True enough, as he was speaking, I felt the touch of his hand fade from mine and everything became sharper, the wind that had been blowing now chilled my skin, the smell of the smoke became stronger, more bitter.

"Where are we?"

"An old memory of mine, nothing important, we won't be here long."

As we walked I noticed two other people some distance away, a man and a boy. The man seemed familiar but the boy was a stranger. As I struggled to read their features I realised why the man triggered in my memory; he was also standing next to me.

"That looks like you," I said as Dallion followed my gaze.

"It was once, time gets a little soft in these places, come on we must keep moving we don't want them to see us that would only complicate matters."

He turned away and began to stroll off at speed; I had to jog a little in order to keep up.

"Where are we going?" I asked.

"To see an oracle of sorts. Someone I used to know who is in the perfect position to give us a little information."

"Where are they?"

"'Straight on 'til morning.'"

"Excuse me?"

"Sorry, space gets a little confusing in these places. Wait."

He stopped suddenly and appeared to sniff the air for something. He then darted right and left, hunting for something beyond my senses. Finally, he stopped and thrust his hand out in mid-air. Everything rippled around his fist, like the surface of a lake after a large stone has been thrown into it. He inserted his other hand and began to pull the fabric of it apart. It was soundless, the stuff of this perceived reality parting with a fluidity that, while clearly hard physical work, was almost natural.

"Come closer to me," he hissed, his teeth gritted against the strain.

I stood behind his shoulder. Through the gap I could see what appeared to be a city street. There was something unusual about it that was hard to place.

"Jump through!"

I leaped forward; there was a bizarre sensation of the air changing around me as I pierced the barrier between these two worlds, then the feel of soft rain on my face as I stood in the street that I had seen through the divide. It was both comfortably familiar and perversely strange. Old Victorian buildings stood side by side with bizarre glass and metal constructions, the cars that lined the kerbsides were small and sleek, recognizable in their basic structures and yet clearly adapted and altered beyond the vehicles I was used to. A bar further down the street was playing loud music, well music of *sorts*, the pumping rhythm of it was much faster and frantic than my ears were used to and there were few instruments that I could recognize, no guitars or voice, just a strange selection of keyboard tones like a Hammond organ playing at the wrong speed.

"Oh brave new world that has such vibe in it," chuckled Dallion as he appeared next to me.

"Where on earth are we?"

"London, several years into your future, it's alright we're perfectly safe."

"We've travelled in time?" My head was full of Wells and Asimov, checking around me for police boxes.

"In a way. What you must appreciate is that time is movable; this is the future as it stands, the most *likely* eventuality. This is the 'current' future. Everything we do can change the world to a degree, small stuff for the most part, although there's always the possibility of apocalypse past every potential. It's tricky stuff to get your head around, I shouldn't worry about it."

But I couldn't help but try; this was every science fantasy I had dreamed of.

"So somewhere in this world I'm all grown up and getting on with my life? There's now two of me in existence?"

"Such confidence, who says you live this long?"

This thought hadn't occurred to me. He looked at me, his eyes softening a little.

"Sorry, that was tactless. Look, it's like I said: the future can always change. At this moment you do exist here, you have a very successful career, a wonderful house and the life you'd always dreamed of. I just don't want you to confuse likelihood with fact, just because you know that this *can* happen doesn't mean you can do whatever you want, risk whatever you want. You're not invulnerable. If you got yourself killed then your future self would wink out of existence and reality slowly shift around to paper over the cracks. I've seen all too many people lulled into a false sense of security by their perceived futures who self-destruct in the misguided notion that they can do what they want. Time just doesn't work like that; it's not looking out for you, it'll change as a direct consequence of what you do."

There is no such thing as destiny; we make our own futures in this life.

"So what is this marvellous career then?" I asked, a smile on my face now.

"You really expect me to tell you that?"

"After dragging me through all reality and getting me drunk I think it's only fair."

He laughed and began to walk up the street.

"As it happens it's pretty safe in your case, there was

never really any doubt, a degree of self confidence would probably help in fact. You're a successful writer."

"Really?"

"Absolutely, oh, you'll slog your guts out getting nowhere for years, that's a given. But, eventually, your first novel is published, everybody loves it and the rest is deadlines."

He looked at me seriously then.

"But remember what I said, just because you know it could happen doesn't mean you don't have to work at it. Get lazy and you'll never get beyond your first short story."

"Point taken."

"Good. Come on then, let's get on with it."

We walked up the street for a few minutes with me still gawping at all the familiar things made strange by passing years. We walked past a record shop and I paused in amazement as I looked at the window display, they were all so small! There were lots of names I didn't recognise but then I spotted Cliff Richard and began to foster some doubts about the musical taste of the future.

"Oh he goes on *forever,*" Dallion chuckled. "Don't worry though, it's not all bad, there's still Bowie."

"What? That weird Space Oddity bloke?"

"Just you wait until Ziggy, you'll love it. Then there's The Stones of course, although they don't record much new stuff."

"What about The Who?" I asked, thinking of my brother and his heroes.

"Hmm. Touchy subject this year. Right, we're here."

We were stood outside a rather imposing Victorian structure that towered over at least five floors, double fronted with a set of impressive stone steps that led to the entrance. A gilt plaque at the foot of the steps announced it as The Vickers Mental Health Institution.

"What's that supposed to mean then?"

"It's an asylum, they just get better at talking round the point in the future."

"This oracle's a nutter?"

"He has his problems, yes, he has a lot in his head you see, too much for safety in fact."

"How do you mean?"

Dallion sighed and sat down on one of the steps.

"I'd forgotten how tiring it is having to explain everything as you go."

I sat down next to him. He reached into his coat and took out a cigar, lit it and took a deep breath.

"By now you will appreciate that there are people in the world that have powers beyond the normal abilities recognised by science. You will also realise that there's a lot more to so called 'reality' than you had previously believed."

"Okay."

"Well, the man we're going to see has the most unique perspective of all. In fact, arguably all of reality is here because of him, lives through him. He is, in some ways, the lynchpin of existence; neither of us can even begin to conceive of the *weight* of that. Everything that happens in any number of realities passes by his attention, which is why we've come to get a few clues as to what we might be dealing with. "

"Sounds to me like you're telling me God lives in a loony bin."

"Would you blame him?"

"That's weird."

"Yet again you cut through the metaphysics admirably, young man. Shall we go inside?"

"To meet God? If I'd known I'd have worn my Sunday best."

"Do you know, you're beginning to get altogether too cocky about all this for my liking."

"What can I say? We award winning authors are very adaptable people."

"Get inside, you cheeky young git."

Just as I was wondering quite how Dallion expected to get through a heavy locked door and, no doubt, several security staff, he veered to the left and with a jolly click of his heels jumped straight through the brick wall. After a moment his head popped back out.

"Well, adaptable author, had you forgotten we're only here in spirit?"

"Of course not," I said, delicately sticking my foot out to see if it would pass through the wall. When the toe met the brick it slipped through and with a kick, it was up to the shin.

"That was my knee you just kicked."

I waggled my finger cheekily into his face and then walked through after him.

On the other side we were in a white room that was desperately trying not to look like the cell it had clearly been built as many years ago. There was a bed in the corner where an elderly woman lay curled, her fingers tapping and pulling nervously at the medical smock she wore. Dallion strolled straight through the bed and beyond the wall on the other side. I followed but couldn't help apologising to the woman as I passed.

"Don't mind me, dear," she said. "You get used to it in my line of business."

I thanked her and carried on my way.

We repeated this several times until Dallion cut through into the adjoining corridor and with a casual wave at a couple of strange looking wall-mounted cameras began to jog up the stairs.

We went all the way up, five floors. Five *bloody* floors, as Sandra would say. In fact by the time we got to the top it was exactly what *I* would have said if keeping up with Dallion hadn't completely robbed me of the ability to breathe. Not noticing an iron lung to hand, or perhaps a small team of trained nurses to coax my respiration back into shape, I waved at Dallion to stop and bent over to get my breath back.

"Being purely spirit should mean I don't get out of breath," I wheezed.

"Your brain's getting confused again, you're being physical so it responds accordingly; try distancing yourself a bit more."

"If I distance myself too much will I fall through the floor?"

"Good point, get your breath back, it's not worth the hassle."

After a moment I stretched up and followed him through a pair of double doors that led onto another long corridor, at the end of which we were faced with a solitary door. The lights were dimmer here, everywhere else had been harsh white but as we walked along I became aware of shadow, faint at first then growing thicker as we reached the end. Dallion halted at the door and tried to peer through the wire glass window inside.

"What are you doing here?" asked a voice behind us.

I spun round expecting to come face to face with a security guard, or doctor perhaps. It was actually a man dressed in the most incongruous set of clothes. He had a vaguely mediaeval look about him: a white smock made from some sort of linen material, wide-open neck threaded with cord; there was a thick leather belt wrapped around his waist with several pouches fixed to it, beneath which he wore modern blue jeans. A black frock-suit jacket, that made him look like a bit of a cowboy, topped off the bizarre combination. His hair was closely cropped which made his young and rather gentle face seem harsher than it otherwise would. His eyes were the most piercing shade of blue I think I've ever seen.

"Just popping by for a visit, show our respects, that sort of thing," said Dallion, stepping forward in a rather confrontational manner.

"I never pictured you as the respectful sort."

"Well, there you are, man of many levels, you know me."

"Yes, I do, I know you very well, which is something you would be advised not to forget."

I sighed and turned to the door.

"If you two have finished sizing each other up, didn't we come here to meet the man?"

"And who might you be?" the strange man asked.

"My name's Greg and I'm possibly drunk, definitely freaked out but most of all very curious about meeting the man on the other side of that door. And you are?"

"The man that's stood *between* you and that door."

"Oh come on!" said Dallion. "You know we don't mean him any harm, for goodness sake. I just want to ask him some questions, that's all."

Suddenly the lights flickered all along the corridor and I felt a strange pulling deep within my gut. I looked over to Dallion and saw him double over. He glanced up at the stranger and rolled his eyes.

"Now then, there's no need to start getting all..."

His words were snatched from him as both of us, ethereal spirits or not, were pulled, with great force, through the wall behind us and into the room beyond it. I felt myself thrust upwards until I came to a decidedly physical stop in the corner of the ceiling. In the faint light shed by a small bedside lamp I could see Dallion in the corner to my left. His coat lashed open, his pack of playing cards floating from his inside pocket and spreading themselves into a fan in front of his face. There was a voice, a strange, quiet tone that I realised came from *inside* my head rather than outside of it.

"Long time no see, Dallion, pick a card..."

Dallion attempted to laugh but the pressure holding him to the roof made it a little difficult.

"Evening, Charlie, how've you been keeping?"

-3.4-

"God's name's Charlie?"

"God's a surname," said the voice in my head. "Joke."

"Ha. Ha," I replied, perhaps a little too sarcastically for the company of a deity. Although, it has to be said, he didn't *look* much like a deity. He wasn't old enough for one thing, mid-fifties or so, frankly insufficient for the 'supreme being'. His hair was white but this was clearly some form of genetic curiosity as it still had all the thick richness of healthy hair. He was quite a small man, suffering from wastage probably; despite the blankets pulled over him his limbs were visibly wiry. There was just something indefinably wrong about him in the God stakes, something that was more instinctual than perceived... something...

Oh all right, his beard was absolutely *rubbish*. Seriously... it was little more than stubble.

The man from outside the room opened the door and joined us, standing protectively at the foot of the man's bed.

"Everything alright, Charlie?" he asked out loud.

"Don't fret so, Lashram, I'm sure they don't mean any harm."

"Thank you for your faith, Charlie," wheezed Dallion.

"Do you think it might extend to letting us stand on our own two feet?"

"If you were so desperate to do that then you wouldn't have come running for my help."

Dallion gritted his teeth and growled slightly.

"Oh very funny..."

We dropped to the floor.

"I'm beginning to think God's a bit moody," I mumbled.

"STOP CALLING ME THAT!" the voice screamed, with enough force to make me cry out in pain. Tapping at my nose I felt a small trickle of blood.

"...and sensitive," I added, rather recklessly in hindsight. I needn't have worried, it would seem his outburst had unnerved him as well. The body in the bed writhed uncomfortably, although it didn't open its eyes. Lashram moved to the side of the bed and stroked the man's brow. After a few seconds the body stopped moving, slumping prostrate again on the bed. Lashram turned to me and, to be fair, there was no anger in his eyes.

"You mustn't agitate him like that, he's... delicate."

Dallion touched me gently on the shoulder and moved to the bedside.

"I'm sorry, Charlie, we probably shouldn't have come. You know me, cutting corners as usual. I just thought you might have been aware of a few titbits of information, a few pointers perhaps. I wouldn't have bothered you but it's killing people... children actually, and I thought anything was worth a try to resolve matters quickly."

"Including an attempt to manipulate my emotions? I'm not sure I have the propensity for guilt or empathy anymore, Magician. There are nations in my skull, endless parades of species, you begin to lose coherence with the smaller stuff after a while."

Dallion sighed and moved away from the bed.

"Worth a try I suppose. Come on, Gregory, let's get on home."

"Wait," the voice whispered. Dallion, his back turned to the bed, smiled rather smugly. "It's from... *outside* of things..."

"Could you be a little more specific?" Dallion asked.

"It's so ethereal, hardly there, little more than an idea. When it strays into the physical it feels like indigestion. A random urge. It wants..."

"What?" said Dallion, rather impatiently.

"That's it, it just wants... it *is* hunger."

"Lovely. Useful." Dallion began to move away again, taking me by the shoulder.

"There is a place like this," the voice continued. "A place for the mentally broken, the desperate and lunatic. Her number's Thirty-Three. She's important."

"The Cliff Tops, mental hospital out of town?" I suggested to Dallion.

"Sounds likely, doesn't it," he nodded. "Either that or a late night Chinese takeaway."

"We'll try the hospital first I think," I suggested.

"Up to you, although when someone dies of a psychotic Chow Mein I hope you can live with yourself."

"So full of yourself," muttered Lashram, herding us from the room.

"At least there's enough of me to be full about," Dallion replied. "See you in a few more years, Charlie, mind how you go."

We left as quickly as we came; the stairs were much easier going down.

"Don't you think we were a bit rude?" I asked as we emerged onto the street.

"Probably, childish really, we have... *history* I suppose you'd say, I sometimes let my emotions get the better of me. Still, at least we've got something to be going along with."

"Oh yes." I rolled my eyes, zombie-like "'*It is hunger!*'"

"Yes, well, bit vague but there you go. It's hard to be specific when you're an ultimate power with the world in your belly."

I sighed, hands in my pockets, glancing in the windows of the shops again.

"He didn't seem that impressive really."

Dallion stopped walking and laughed.

"You'll change your mind in a few years, lad, he's what your first book's about."

I stopped too.

"My novel's about him?"

"*The Imagineer*, yes, you write it as a gift, others like it and before you know it everybody loves the book that you weren't that fussed about yourself."

I smiled.

"And Gregory Ashe becomes a household name!"

"Nice to know that you can keep art in perspective."

Bugger art; give me fame every time.

"Come on. 'Home again, home again...'"

-3.5 -

"'...Jiggety Jig!'"

We were back in the room at Sandra's house. The air was suffocating compared to the breeze of the outside streets. Although, as I hadn't physically been outside, that was probably my mind playing tricks more than anything else.

"This place is such a tip," muttered Dallion, looking around. "I may have to have words with the landlady."

"She could kill you with one lash of her tongue. I wouldn't try it," I suggested, trying to shift the pins and needles from my legs. "How long have we been gone? My legs are killing me."

Dallion pulled the curtains apart, the sun had moved on, late afternoon, possibly even evening. I checked my watch in the light. Four hours had passed.

"I'd better ring home, tell them I'm with Sandra."

"If you really think that would reassure them. Then, we must be getting on with more important things."

"What, you want to go to the asylum now?"

"God no, I'm starving. I was thinking of fish and chips."

We dashed downstairs chuckling, although any sense of cheerfulness died the moment we entered the living room. I think it was the only time I saw Sandra crying. She was still sat in her armchair, although the cards were now littered on the floor.

"What's wrong?" I asked.

"Jesus, Gregory, it's that poor kid they found naked on the beach. Jessica, y'know. It's in the paper." She flung the local paper towards me. "Apparently she tried to kill her parents the night after they found her."

"Jessica?" I couldn't believe what she was saying; she was so *young* for God's sake.

"Attacked them with a kitchen knife while they slept."

"You said 'tried' to kill them," Dallion mumbled, scratching his head in thought.

"They're both alright, well, *physically*. Her father's got a shoulder wound I think but that's about it. The paper doesn't go into much detail. The story only came out at all because one of the orderlies has been talking."

"Orderlies?" I asked.

"They took her to The Cliff Tops; the poor sod's been sat in an asylum ever since."

FOUR

What a ridiculous species we are.

Never has this been clearer than in our foolish obsession for pattern and mythical framework. As we huddle together on our spinning ball of mud we gaze up at the stars, feeling coldly insecure by their sheer size and scale, by their automatic suggestion of our minimal significance. There is nothing we like more than the belief of a shape to it all, that we will one day make sense.

We see gods in snowflakes, mystic messages in the bowls of our beverage containers, bristling stigmata in the cold porous flesh of statuettes.

Somewhere in Idaho tonight a family will weep openly at the perceived face of Jesus within the weave of a bath towel or dishcloth, blind to the mundane facts of caked on fat molecules or sweat stains. This will not be a sign of the coming.

And no amount of genuflection towards the sink is going to make it so.

None of which counts for a damn, however, when we also appreciate that life has one other constant: it likes its irony cut cake thick.

Or, put another way, sometimes the patterns *are* there.

We just don't see them.

**Joe Rigby remembers how cold it is
in the sea's heart.**

Between mouthfuls of cheap rum and a pipe as rough as if it were filled with the pubic hair of a horse, he casts his mind back. He has the unfortunate handicap of being younger than he looks, but then, after years of self-abuse and a skin almost completely reliant on the perpetual crust of salt to keep it on his bones, it is no great surprise. He has yet to hit sixty, though he won't be able to say this for long (and, the way he's going, the time he has left will be more than adequate to thrash his internal organs to the point of collapse with weeks to spare). His duties of maintaining the lifeboat and other council holdings are mundane at best, but he's been here most of his life so has at least one factor in common with the limpets he is paid to strip from the dark wood of the boat's hull : he is incredibly bloody stubborn.

One could also say he lacks backbone but that would be treading somewhat personally and you might find that, if riled, Rigby has backbone aplenty. He just keeps it in reserve for special occasions, someone touching his drink; y'know, the *important* stuff.

Not that he hasn't seen action on the waves, he's been known to go out with the crew every now and then, dipped his toe so to speak. There was that time in '54, for instance, when Jimmy King was doubled up with the squits and someone had to haul the regatta banners back in after some wag had severed their knots on the pier. He'd been on board then, boat hook in hand and pulling his weight with the boys (until a stray wave had given the boat an almighty shove and sent him overboard – much to the hilarity of the others). There was also that time in '48 but he doesn't like to go into that, no matter how much rum has passed his cracked lips.

No, he's done his job but no more, likes to keep the deck light, so to speak.

Not that he doesn't have responsibility. He has the maintenance of the boat and its rigging, the general upkeep of the sheds and, for the last few days, there is a responsibility locked inside his personal tool shed that he takes very seriously indeed.

On the subject of which, he thinks, glancing at the battered old pocket watch his father gave him when there was still hope for a bright future, *feeding time.*

-4.3-

I hope I die before I get old,

Jeremy Ashe thinks to himself as he empties his bladder in the alley behind the club, a head full of leapers, cash on the hip and a battered pack of Woodbines he's stolen in the pocket of his parka. The old bastard behind the bar is still complaining about their set, no doubt, full of all the righteous indignation of a man to whom rebellion is nothing but a dim and distant memory. He won't pay, Jeremy is fully aware of the fact, whatever the kids thought of it, whatever the bar take, the bastard won't pay. And, just as soon as he's got his scooter on the road, tanked up and London bound he'll make sure he leaves the git something to remember him by.

Jeremy's got a future, knows it everyday he looks in the mirror, knows it when he puts the firm creases in his Italian shirt and runs his fingers along the lapels of his Zoot Suit. Knows it whenever he feels that swell from the cheap amp as his thumb knocks out a power chord. Oh yes, Jeremy has a future; it lasts just as long as his mid-twenties, beyond that... blessed oblivion.

He zips up his fly, ruffles his coat into shape, lights a cigarette with all the finesse of a pro and walks back to the lamplight and the band.

"Who's up for a drink and a smoke then?" he asks, for all the world a man of substance who doesn't live with his parents and has set foot outside town with more frequency than the occasional school trip.

It's Keith's turn; renting a cheap cellar bed-sit in a house full of absentees has its advantages after all. They all pile in after a brief stop at Joan's house to half inch a two-thirds bottle of gin from her mother's cabinet and, within the hour, Jeremy's got his mouth round the bottle and wondering if Joan's got something in her knickers that might take his mind of the sour taste of cheap booze. Learn to share the drink a bit and he might just find out.

Keith's lying flat on the floor, a folded up copy of the New Musical Express as a pillow, and Jeremy can tell from the look on his face that he's thinking about pushing for a change from bass, maybe a bit of lead guitar work. That just won't do. Not that he's not capable, he's got a natural flair for fretwork, but Jeremy's damned if he's going to share the limelight. It's a common argument between them, and it'll come to the point where Jeremy will be forced to back down or kick off, until then he relies on Dave to act as mediator, the rhythm section's on his side after all, he's promised it a lift to London and a new life just as soon as he's got the bike up and running.

He looks around for Dave, it's amazing that in such a small room he can stay hidden for any length of time but it's a few moments before he realises that Ann didn't go 'for a lie down' on her own. Dirty little slapper, he thinks, lying to himself that its got anything to do with the fact that they had a quick fumble of their own under the pier a few months ago. Ann's been hanging around them for months, their own little groupie; it's her that drags along friends from school to fill out the crowds. Friends like Joan.

Friends like Lisa.

Jeremy takes another mouthful of gin and stares intently at the front of Jean's sweater; it doesn't bulge much but there's enough to pique his interest. She's blonde at least; he likes blondes, decent legs too, from what he can see beneath the hem of her skirt. Might be worth a spin. A quick once round the waltzers.

"Have a drink, love," he says passing the bottle and a head full of promises. 'Nice and smooth' as Ray would say.

"Got something better than that," mumbles Keith, ferreting in his jacket pocket. "Scored some Acid from Derek at the Anchor."

"Bollocks, knowing that cowboy you've got nothing but horse pills."

"Derek's alright, 'sides, it's not pills, is it?"

Jeremy chooses just to tut; much to his embarrassment he knows little about these things. Still, anything that might loosen that bulging woollen sweater.

"Divvy it up then, you tight bastard."

"Pay your way and I might consider it."

"Watch it, pal, just remember who it was that paid for those new strings of yours, hand over the goods and let's be having less lip."

Keith sighs and presses a couple of tabs into his hand, one each.

"I don't know about that," mutters Joan, but he can tell she doesn't mean it, not enough to refuse him anyway, she still has a star struck glimmer in her eyes.

"Just lie back and think of England darlin,'" he says, popping the square piece of paper under her tongue. Hmm, nice mouth, he thinks as he lies back, realising that at the right angle he can see straight up her skirt.

Nice and smooth...

-4.4-

One day, he thinks, this will be nothing but memory...

Though, by Lord, that makes it no easier. Stood here on the deserted sand he would be naught but a stranger to those that know him, no... know his *reputation*; there are truly none that know *him*. Even his dear Eliza, who weeps behind him, folded into her bath chair like an early invalid, the coarse hand of her nurse resting on the black lace of her shawl in a pretence of understanding and consolation. Yes, even her. She sees only as much as he is willing to show. More than the fellows from his club perhaps, more than his many investors certainly but never the whole, never the complete Joshua Walgrave.

This is how he became the man he is.

And now all he has to show for it lies curled in the small pine box at his feet, a box too small by far. He feels that he would gladly trade all of his trappings, the spa, the hotel, the plans and burgeoning buildings, the half finished pier that juts out into the water to his left, yes all of these beginnings of his town. *His* town. Trade all of that just for the smallest breath on those pale blue lips. It might even be true, although in the years to come, as the emotion fades and his fortunes continue to grow, he will question it and the guilt will chew him deeply.

Behind him he can hear his Spaniel in the grass of the dunes, yapping at some small discovery in the undergrowth, some small creature, a crab perhaps. To be that oblivious he thinks, and hates the beloved pet a little for it, pure jealousy. The barking is the only noise here, winter is hard upon them and he has closed the hotel and spa for a few weeks, unable to bear the thought of strangers invading them as he looks on the cold remains of his own flesh and blood. It will damage his reputation a little, but not enough to last, there's too much money in the city that itches to be spent out here in the paradise he's built. Fortunes will always fall on Xanadu and a temporary fluctuation in its hospitality will be soon forgotten.

He sighs and drops to his haunches to pick up the box. By Christ, it's light, he can hold it in one hand as he walks to the small rowboat at the water's edge. Behind him he can hear his wife's tears begin to build, the actuality of what he's about to do taking hold of her. He loathes such displays of emotion but, as he feels tears of his own dampen his cheeks, he cannot think ill of her for it. They have earned these tears, let them cry; let them fill the sea with grief.

He places the box inside the boat and begins to push the boat into the swell. The waves lap at his legs, drenching his trousers and the tails of his jacket; let it all be ruined, he'll never wear the suit again after today, let the staff dispose of it howsoever they wish.

He climbs into the boat, struggling for a moment to keep his balance, he's not used to this; lowering himself to the seat awkwardly, grappling for the oars, this is something he's never had to do for on his own, but he'll learn, this is his business and he's damned if he'll do it any other way than alone. Slowly he finds the bite of the paddles in the water, pulling out into the tide. His arms ache from the work but that's probably good, he feels so numb that a degree of pain doesn't go amiss.

After a few minutes he glances over his shoulder at the shore, now a goodly distance away, far enough, he thinks, aware of his selfishness, aware that his wife should be in the boat with him. Aware, but incapable of changing how he feels.

He's careful not to let the oars slip into the water - he has no wish to be stranded out here, finishing the day in considerable ignominy as he waits for rescue. No, he will do this precisely and methodically; take some small piece of pride in being able to see to his affairs without the assistance of others. He picks up the box and wonders whether he should open it one last time.

Can he bear to look upon its contents once more? Then a thought occurs to him, the watch he wears, the watch given to him upon his eighteenth birthday. There's no doubt in his mind that he would have passed it on when the time was right. Now will just have to do, let it be the weight that carries the box to the deep.

He opens the box, biting his lip at the urge to scream as he looks upon the cold flesh, and drops the watch inside. He closes the lid.

"Happy Birthday."

Leaning over carefully he places the box into the water, pushing it down so that the sea begins to flow into the holes he drilled into its sides, filling it, consuming it. He lets go and watches as the box canters in the tide, sinking slowly, down and down until, just below the surface, it vanishes, to carry on the journey on its own.

He supposes he should say a prayer, but for the life of him he can't think of anyone he would want to pray to, so he just picks up the oars and begins the return journey to shore.

-4.5-

Just a Travelin' Man...

...a cool talkin', hip-swingin', gun smoking,' cat riding the light fantastic.

Time loss.

The colours are brighter than they should be

(or the reverse, maybe he's always seen them too dull and is only now seeing them in full frequency, hi-fidelity spectrum).

Jesus, the carpet's making his eyes bleed, there's no way red should be that... well... *red*.

Joan's flat on her back, writhing, hair splayed like a fountain of blonde, he can see sweat on her thighs. Hmm... Little wet pearls, glistening, bright. He can feel her heat, taste it in his head. He tries to reach her but he's not sure if he's moving or not, it feels like it but his perspective doesn't seem to change. *Push.*

That's it, forward momentum, forwards, forwards, forwards...

Focus on the beads of sweat, pick one, enlarge it, follow it as it slides across the pale skin, curled in the slipstream. Shooting upwards, inwards.

Inside (*oh God*) there she is; he can taste the salt, hear the rushing of water, feel it splash against his cheeks. There is the roar of the wave and he's in the ocean, lost at sea... (*am I drowning?*) No. Not drowned, afloat, firm hands on his shoulders. Voices in his ear. Giving him directions, telling him stories.

He can see things, distant things... a cinema show with a hammered projector, hunting for focus. There is a world of black sand, smoke furls in the sky. Then there is a fan of playing cards lit by the dull amber glow of a cigar cherry. Then a man in a boat, dressed in fancy dress, sepia photo clothes, small box in his hand. Then dark brick walls (*33 is laughing/crying*) and the sound of muted screams. Back on the beach the sea freezes, becoming static peaks solid enough to walk on. The smell of greasepaint.

The voice carries on in his ear, whispering plans, making suggestions.

The beach: flat and unmarked, the sea: brittle glass bright and unmoving. He is sat cross-legged on the sand listening to the voice in his head. In front of him a man comes into view, his suit sharp as a razor, parka slung open, hair flat and trimmed, a thing of beauty. It's only as the man cups a cigarette in his hand and lights it that he recognizes him, sees beyond the faint lines of aging, the delicate web of creases around the eyes and the corner of the mouth. This paragon of the modern world is *him* with a few more years on the speedometer.

"Evenin', old son," says his older self. "Lookin' sharp,

feelin' sharp?"

"Guess so,"

"Pleased to hear it, you've got a little business ahead of you and I need to know you're up to the job."

"You know it."

"That's my boy, going to shake things up a bit, show the town how we do things in this generation. Teach a few important lessons. You happy to bring a bit of the old Whitsun Holiday fun to the streets?"

"Say the word,"

"You'll know it."

He throws his cigarette towards the sea where it bounces and rolls a couple of times before coming to rest under the hang of a particularly prominent wave. He begins to walk away along the beach, pauses for a second, turns.

"Give 'er one from me, eh?"

He winks and vanishes.

And, as the beach melts and resolves slowly into Keith's living room once more, Jeremy pulls himself across to lean over Joan, gazing down at that lovely little woollen sweater and all it might be hiding. He loosens his tie, puts a sweating hand on her exposed thigh and says:

"I might just do that."

-4.6-

Jeffery Collins knows that less is more but, damn it, with lashes like these it would be a crime to hold back.

He shifts the angle of the mirror to better catch the light, painting the mascara as thick as he can without losing definition. God, but you're gorgeous, he thinks as he clicks the cap back in place, placing the pot back in his special case and reaching for a particularly outrageous shade of lipstick.

Such a tart!

For a moment he wonders what people would think

if they could see him now, dreadful police uniform shed to be transformed into this radiant glamour doll. Ladies and gentlemen, behold the luscious long legs of the law.

He chuckles then curses in a decidedly unladylike manner as he smudges the lipstick. It's as he's reaching for a tissue that he notices the reflection in the mirror doesn't move with him, rather smiles lovingly and flutters its beautiful lashes in his direction. This comes as something of a shock, all things considered, and he knocks over the Chanel Number 5 that Julia bought him for his last birthday.

Good old Julia, surprise confidante Julia, he knows they all think that the ticket booth girl and he are an item and, in truth, they were for a few months. Then she caught him trying on her rouge. He had been terrified at the time, convinced that she would scream in shock and run out of the house determined to tell the world that the local constabulary had a weakness for makeup and silk underwear. She had simply sighed, brushed his hand away, taken the brush and begun applying the makeup for him. He had cried, the tears smudging the makeup dreadfully. Ever since, she had been the only person that knew his secret, helped him buy new colours and shades, acting as his perfect cover. There was nothing physical in their relationship, that was clearly a little uncomfortable for her, but they were inseparably close nonetheless and he loved her dearly. Dear sweet Julia...

The face in the mirror was still looking at him, even as he tried to mop at the spilled scent. He really didn't know how to react; it was too bizarre to truly register. He swayed from side to side, disturbed at the stillness of his reflection. Disturbed even more when she began to speak.

"Darling, you look marvellous, don't stop there, perhaps a little more eye shadow?"

Jeffery gave a startled cry and held his hand to his mouth, subconsciously confirming it remained closed.

"Careful love, you'll smudge your lipstick."

That cinched it, his hand had been firmly on his lips, they hadn't moved at all, it was his voice certainly, albeit in the higher pitch he had often caught himself affecting when he was dressed up. Slowly he moved his hand away, automatically dabbing at his lips with a tissue to repair any damage.

"That's better darling, we need to look our best now don't we? We don't want people thinking we're cheap."

"People?"

"Oh yes... I think it's time we showed the world, don't you?"

Jeffery feels his heart trip, pounding in instinctual fear. There were a number of rules he applied to his predilections, never stoop to Rimmel and never, *never*, let anyone catch him 'clothed'. The second was almost certainly the more important of the two (although 'making do' with cheap slap was an absolute kick in the teeth).

"I really don't think..."

"Shhh. Now look at yourself, look properly. Have you ever seen anything more beautiful? Ever seen anything more perfect? Where's your wig?"

Jeffery pulls out a lower draw in the bureau and lifts out his full blonde 'bob', brushing it through carefully before slipping it over his scalp.

"There you go, tease it and ease it baby, ooh *gorgeous.*"

He feels his usual swell of pride, the warm flood just under the skin, the fine hairs on his arms prickling with excitement as he gazes upon his real face.

"Now get dressed."

He slips on his favourite red silk blouse, running his hands across the false mounds of the padded bra beneath the fabric, then pulls up his black skirt over thick stockings, tucking in the blouse and smoothing the skirt over his childbearing hips.

"Perfect, perhaps a dab of that sublime scent... Now, tell me what could be more wonderful than that?"

He poses in front of his full-length mirror, slipping on his heels and spinning the foot on the point. You know, she was quite right; it would be a crime not to show this beauty to the world.

"Come on, tiger, show 'em what you've got!"

He throws his head back and gives the mirror his best Bardot stare, blows his reflection a kiss and turns to leave.

"Hang on a moment, love, it's a bit chilly out, you might want your fur coat. Go the whole hog, love, knock 'em dead!"

He pulls his coat out of the back of the wardrobe, drapes it round his shoulders and pulls it tight, his upper arms creating a small enhanced cleavage. Oooh you sexy beast! Hips rolling and sensuous he leaves his bedroom and walks down the stairs, careful on his heels.

For a moment he pauses at the door as he hears the quiet voice inside him, the public voice, the policeman's voice, the voice of Jeffery Collins.

"Jesus, you sure about this?"

"Just you watch, darling, leave it to Lola, they won't know what hit them!"

Lola Collins hits the streets at just after eight...

-4.7-

Suited and booted, the boys are abroad.

Jeremy looks the business and knows it, by God. To his left Keith tightens his tie, to his right Dave shoots out an extra half inch of cuff. The town won't know what hit it, the pavements clicking to the rhythmic tap of top quality Italian heels.

They head towards the pier looking for action...

-4.8-

Lola Collins kisses the breeze as it caresses her perfectly painted cheeks.

She gazes out to sea, leaning back against the railing of the pier, letting the wind pass through her clothes. Hotter than the sun and twice as blinding. She sees the boys heading her way; can't blame them, moths to a flame. They haven't been the first, she'd seen the heads turn all the way along the high street as she stepped in and out of the spotlights of the streetlamps. A group of lads had thrown her a wolf whistle as they stepped into The Anchor for a jar; she had giggled and blown them a kiss leaving them wanting more. There's something about these three that gives her pause though, its not just the Mod suits and coats, not just the arrogant swagger as they head over to where she's standing. It's something in their eyes, furious little piss holes in the snow.

"Out for a little action, are we boys?" she asks, trying to hide some of her nervousness. The one in the middle glances to his left as if listening to someone else, though there's nobody there that she can see; he cocks his head though, definitely listening to something...

"That's right, mate, you want some?" he sneers eventually, just before they wade in.

The first punch smears a streak of Max Factor and spittle across her left cheek, a kick to the groin sends her to her hands and knees where she sheds a couple of false nails. Then there's a kick to the head and the Mary Quant eyeliner clashes with the red eruption as her nose pops with blood and snot. Christ, she's looking a mess...

All three weigh in with punches and kicks, the final indignation coming as the smell of her Chanel is drowned beneath the embarrassing stench of her bladder voiding involuntarily, the urine burning on her thighs as it soaks into her skirt and the delicate material of her stockings.

She begins to cry as they hold her up against the railings, her wig hanging loose to one side of her head. The leader of the pack pulls it from her head and begins to cram it into her mouth where the blood from split lips seeps into the beautiful blonde strands and sullies them. She bites down on his fingers, feeling a glorious crunch of knuckle as her jaw clamps down. He yells and pulls back his hand.

"Stupid cunt!" he shouts and with a roar puts out one of her eyes with the index finger of his other hand.

It's through a haze of blood and optic fluid that she sees them circle her as she slumps to the floor, sees them move in again to lift her up and over the railing, sees the sky spiral as she tumbles backwards over the metal bar and falls all the way down into the cold sea below.

She dies with a lungful of blood and saltwater, a

solitary high heeled shoe bobbing on the waves like a small child's toy boat.

-4.9-

Joe Rigby almost cries at her beauty as he tears off a chunk of salmon paste sandwich and puts it in her mouth.

In the distance he is vaguely aware of the sound of shouting and then a loud splash as something falls off the pier but it barely registers; here in his shed the world beyond the damp treated wood slat walls has ceased to exist.

He found her floating in the shallows three nights ago, transfixed by the beauty of her golden hair, pale white skin, the delicate mounds of her breasts, the way the moonlight sparkles off the aquamarine glimmer of the scales in her tail. The most beautiful thing he's ever seen. No question.

He keeps her wet, dousing her with seawater regularly enough to keep the sparkle of her tail alive. He feeds her from his lunchbox whenever he knows they're alone. He wishes he didn't have to keep her chained but the brutal and selfish part of him doesn't want to let something so wonderful go. He coos reassurance to her whenever he holds her, she never speaks back, probably can't speak, but she seems to take the food willingly enough, and, when he can't resist the urge, she never resists his kisses.

Joe Rigby might just be in love...

FIVE

"'By the pricking of my thumbs...'"

"Excuse me?" I asked. We were in Sandra's back garden, Dallion standing in the centre of the small lawn, a blossom of fish and chip paper in his left hand, ketchup covered chip in the right; caught halfway between paper and mouth. He froze like that for a moment, sniffing the air. Then, suddenly, he snapped to attention, glancing down at his chip in slight confusion for a second before tossing it into his mouth. After a few seconds of chewing he seemed to remember that I was out there with him as he turned and smiled a little.

"'By the pricking of my thumbs, something wicked this way comes.' It's a quote."

"Shakespeare."

"Ray Bradbury, I think you'll find," he grinned. "It's just an impression, a feeling, there's something unpleasant in the wind tonight." He looked pensive all of a sudden. "Things may be coming to a head quicker than we'd like. Finish your chips, we'll visit The Cliff Tops tonight."

"Tonight?" I nearly choked on a chip.

"Well, the way we're getting in makes visiting hours a touch irrelevant, the sooner the better. Things are rattling along here, barely a pause for breath."

"You're suggesting we break in?"

Dallion laughed and took a vicious bite of his fish.

"What else did you have in mind, knocking on the door and asking for five minutes of the girl's time? I think a little stealth's in order, don't you?"

Sandra chose that moment to stumble out of the door, cursing loudly as she tripped over next-door's cat, showering it in soggy chips as it ran for cover.

"We'll be wanting Sandra on board then?" I asked, stifling a laugh.

"Absolutely vital I'd say," replied Dallion, completely deadpan.

"You can all shut your faces," hissed Sandra, picking bits of batter from her hair. "Anyway," she added, once satisfied she cut a slightly more authoritative figure, "I fail to see quite what we hope to achieve by hunting down a poor crazed child."

Dallion fidgeted with his chips for a moment.

"It's a little distasteful I know, but she's the only person we know who has come into contact with whatever it is out there. It would be foolish not to try and get some information out of her."

"And how exactly do you propose going about it?"

Dallion threw his chips to the floor.

"I don't know! Haven't got a clue! I'm making this up as I go along, as if that wasn't painfully obvious. And, frankly, if you have no constructive suggestions I'd appreciate it if you'd let me get on with it."

There was a pause as Sandra and he stared at one another. Out of the corner of my eye I saw next-door's cat leap over the wall back to its own territory, deciding it had had enough of these lunatic humans who shouted and threw their food around.

"That was a bit childish wasn't it?" said Sandra.

"Yes it was a bit." Dallion sighed and looked down at his fish and chips. "I was really enjoying those." He dropped to his haunches and tried to salvage what he could.

"Well," I said, "if you've both quite finished, I think we should look to getting ready."

"Quite right," replied Dallion, blowing grass off a chip.

"Can I wear a balaclava?" asked Sandra.

"Now who's being childish?" Dallion said around a mouthful of recovered chips. Suddenly his face contorted. "Oh bugger, I think I've just eaten an earthworm."

-5.2-

"Do you have a gear for between light speed and emergency halt?

"You know," Dallion added, "something along the lines of 'Won't Kill Passengers While Navigating Quiet Country Roads.'"

"Do you want to drive?" replied Sandra, slamming the gear stick into fourth with the sort of gentility Voodoo Witchdoctors often reserve for chickens. She had changed into black jumper and trousers but had, thankfully, drawn the line at balaclavas.

"There's always a first time, doesn't look difficult, ignore the gears until the engine screams and push the pedals as hard as possible without actually putting your foot through the chassis. I mean, don't get me wrong, as a novice I'll probably keep the speed a bit low, less than three figures say."

"Stick it up your..."

"Sorry! Can't hear you, I think that was the sound barrier back there!" He rifled in the glove box and pulled out the driver's manual. "Would you like me to read you this? Maybe it'll give you a few clues for bringing us down safely."

"If you're still holding that by the time I count to ten I'll put it *in* you."

"Dear God, it's like travelling with a pair of children," I piped up from the back seat.

"Keep it down, Sandra," Dallion chuckled. "Daddy's getting angry."

"You started it!"

I sighed and tried to tell where we were. The asylum was a couple of miles outside town, distant enough to feel isolated yet close enough to still have the most inflammatory residents talk of being murdered in the night by lunatics.

It was an imposing pile of Gothic architecture, salt battered and strewn with the shit from seagulls. Originally a hotel and health spa built by town founder Joshua Walgrave in the latter part of the nineteenth century, it had closed its doors to the wealthy health seekers after his wife had suffered some form of mental breakdown. Rather than send her away to another hospital he had adapted the facilities already in place and 'The Cliff Tops Spa and Retreat' had become simply 'The Cliff Tops' home to the mentally rather than physically infirm.

Have you ever noticed how the more serious the mental patients the more whitewashed the name of the facility that houses them? As if the very name of the building is an attempt to brush their many and various neuroses under some form of semantic carpet. To acknowledge the name would be to endorse the illness.

Still, 'The Cliff Tops' is undoubtedly catchier than something more literal. 'St. Be'Jeezus Home For Chronic Dribblers' would have a rather negative connotation to it.

When I was younger, kids had dared one another to clamber over the gates here and bang on the front door; as if it were some form of haunted house, which I suppose it was, albeit haunted by the living. It was probably still a popular jaunt during summer months; I was just too old for an invite. Thinking back on it, it did seem ridiculous. The residents would have found the presence of an unruly kid on their doorstep far more disturbing than the slim risk we took of being caught. It's all about perspective, I suppose. Not something kids are famous for possessing.

"Where are we?" I asked.

"Judging by our speed, just south of Turkey," Dallion muttered before receiving a vicious slap on his arm from Sandra.

"Nearly there," she said. "It's just up ahead, do you think I should pull in early?"

"That would be plan A," suggested Dallion. "Plan B involves smashing a Maxi through the front gates, I'll leave it to a vote."

Sandra pulled over immediately.

"So much for democracy."

We got out of the car and began to make our way towards the building ahead. There were spotlights on the wall that shone on the building making it look like a prison; which, in many ways is exactly what it was. The driveway cut right from the main road, heading straight towards the edge of the cliffs, and was lined by lamps to keep the cars straight and safe on their route towards the entrance. The roar of the sea was loud, the wind much stronger here right on the coast. I tried to remember the layout of the place from my brief visits. The building was deep and rectangular, with a large gravel entrance court to the front and elongated garden tapering left, away from the cliff's edge at the rear. A large brick wall surrounded it even though the right hand side of the building ran almost adjacent to the rock drop and the sea below. If I remembered correctly there was a small trail of maybe six feet in width that ran along the outermost edge, but that was all the grace offered: beyond that fresh air and a sticky end. After a few more years of erosion no doubt even that small margin would weather away until, eventually, the whole lot would topple into the waves. To the left of the building there was a large plot of open land before it met the main road once again and moved inland.

"So, what would plan A entail exactly?" I asked Dallion, hoping for a cunning arrangement of stealth and meticulous planning.

"Jump over the wall, run like hell and don't be seen."

"I don't suppose we might want to give a degree of thought towards the notion of a plan C?"

"I hate over planning, best to keep it loose, improvise a bit. Think Jazz-style jailbreak... in reverse."

"Maybe I should wait in the car," Sandra muttered while lighting a cigarette.

"If you like, although that would certainly be the most dangerous place to be."

"Really?"

"No, but I can't in all honesty think of a better excuse to keep you with us. You never know though, looks like it could be wolf country, why take unnecessary risks?"

"Good effort, okay I'll stay with you two."

"Glad to hear it."

It seemed to me that there was a small hole in our plan, somewhere near the size of Asia. I thought it best to mention it up front.

"It's all very well to get as far as the building and not be seen but how on earth are we supposed to get inside without someone noticing us? There's bound to be night staff and I don't expect to find many trees, bushes and other natural cover along the corridors."

"Aha!" Dallion grinned. "It just so happens I have got a plan for that bit: *Keep your head down*."

By now we'd reached the wall to the right of the gate.

"Keep your hands on the wall as we move around. There's plenty of space to walk as long as we're careful." He began to lead the way.

"Jesus, why don't we just walk round the other

side?" Sandra flicked her cigarette away and I watched the small ember float forward then vanish as it fell past the cliff edge.

"We're more covered, this side of the building's in shadow. If we follow the path to the rear of the house we should be able to hop over and find a service entrance or some such."

"I trust you noticed his use of the word 'should' in that sentence, Gregory," hissed Sandra.

"I wasn't going to mention it."

We made our way along the path, the wind coming in off the sea proving more of a psychological hindrance than a physical one; as Dallion had said, there was more than enough room to manoeuvre.

As we moved past the building itself I thought I heard wailing and crying from the windows above but it was more than likely just my imagination having a cruel natured laugh at my expense. This is not to say that, with hindsight, the residents didn't have cause for the odd scream now and then just that the windows were probably too thick to let us hear it.

Soon enough we were at the rear of the building and Dallion drew us close.

"Now then," he said with a grin far more genuine than it had any real right to be, "I suppose you all think I'm going first don't you?"

"Damn right," said Sandra.

"Fair enough." And with that he turned, jumped, and grabbed at the top of the wall. After a deep breath he yanked himself upward, swung his leg over and laid flat across the top edge. He took a moment to glance around on the other side before lowering his head to us slightly. "All clear, who's next?"

Sandra cursed and made an ungainly leap at the wall, Dallion grabbed at her hands while I pushed her legs.

"What do you think this is, the Famous bloody Five?" she whispered, giving my hands a slight kick. "I'm more than capable, thank you."

"Suit yourself," I replied after she had pulled herself over, taking one more quick glance around before I jumped up to join them.

We dropped to the other side as quietly as we could

and moved into the shadow of the building.

There was a small patio garden that looked a little worse for wear but had probably been a thing of beauty when it had still been tended regularly, and a pair of double doors in the centre of the building led to some form of communal dining room. Again this had, no doubt, been an opulent room once where the wealthy guests of Walgrave had gathered to eat their healthy yet lavish food in comfort. Now it was little more than a canteen, for staff or patients I couldn't tell. Several feet further there was a smaller door that probably led into the kitchens. Dallion gestured toward it with his head and we all moved on tiptoe past the large windows, thankful that they were dark. Indeed, the only sign of life at the rear was a single light burning on one of the upper floors, it was this and the light of the moon that guided us past the several overgrown stone planters and weathered statues littering the patio.

Once we were all gathered by the door Dallion pulled us into a tight huddle.

"Do you have one of your especially clever plans to get the door open? Should I have brought a sledgehammer?" asked Sandra.

"It would have matched your wit." Dallion pulled a strangely twisted piece of thin metal from his coat pocket and began to quietly ferret in the keyhole with it. After a few seconds he sighed and looked up at Sandra. "Are you wearing a bra with under-wiring?"

"Yes, don't tell me you expect me to take it off!"

There was a faint click from the door lock.

"Up to you, just wondering that was all." He winked and opened the door.

The room beyond was pitch black but the smell of fat and cooking lingered enough to know that we'd been right in assuming it the kitchen. The air smelt like gravy had been poured all over it and then allowed to congeal.

"If anyone fancies a sandwich, now would be the time to say," whispered Dallion before striding straight into the darkness as if taking a stroll in a park at midday. Sandra and I moved more carefully, afraid of knocking something over or just flying arse over tit when coming nose to nose with a stove. I grabbed her hand and we made in the direction that Dallion had disappeared into. When a crack of light appeared from an opening doorway to our left my immediate reaction was to manfully scream like a girl until I realised that it was Dallion and our direction was just a little off.

"I wasn't being serious, come on it's this way."

He peered out of the door and, after gesturing that it was safe to follow, vanished again.

"So much for keeping together," Sandra sighed as we skipped to catch up with him.

The door opened on a corridor leading to the canteen on our left and a large pair of double doors to our right. The doors were glass panelled at the top showing a similar corridor beyond. Careful not to slip on the polished tile floor (a rather foolhardy construction in my opinion – unless it had been created specifically to cause amusement for the staff as the residents slipped and bounced off the walls at every mealtime) we joined Dallion at the doors.

"There must be a specific area for the more troubled cases, my guess is that we'll find her there," he said, pushing the door open.

"You think?" Sandra whispered sarcastically. "And where would that be?"

"Well, logic would dictate that we go up, they'd keep the ground floor for communal areas, and then stack the patients in order of their ability to actually get around. I doubt the really bad cases tend to leave their rooms."

"I can go along with that," I offered, more to sound constructive than anything else.

"Good, then if we keep on straight we should find a staircase."

"Or... Victorian building, large and, at one time at least, very well to do; might there not be a service stairway?" suggested Sandra.

Dallion looked at her with genuine affection on his face.

"You see, that's why we need you along. With your brains and his beauty we'll be in and out in no time."

"I'm just wondering why we brought you," Sandra smiled and gestured for him to lead the way.

"I make you look good," he chuckled and stepped through the door.

The corridor turned into a crossroads a little way along at which he turned left and, hands in his pockets, strolled on, looking to all the world as if he owned the place.

Sandra and I moved quickly to keep pace as he pushed through another set of double doors and on to a single doorway at the far end which lead onto a narrow stairway.

"Anytime now would be good for an 'I told you so,'" he said, opening the door for us to follow him inside.

We slipped past him and up the stairs.

"All the way to the top?" I asked.

"Why not," he replied. "We can always backtrack if my guess is off."

Stairs again then; bloody stairs. Within the space of two days I had dashed up two long flights of stairs in two mental asylums occupying two time zones. Much more of this and they were going to have to put me in one. Given a choice I would prefer the one from the future, there was something vaguely unpleasant about The Cliff Tops, an atmosphere more than anything tangible. The building was attractive enough; even the service stairway had more sense of aesthetic worth than the interior of The Vickers Institute where we had met Charlie, the stairs were carpeted and the walls were cream rather than the harsh antiseptic white of the former establishment. Perhaps it was purely because I was here in body, but there was a definite discomfort in the pit of my stomach, a tinge of nausea, as if the air here wasn't all that good for you. Maybe my imagination was poking fun again, all I can say is that within those walls I felt captured, pent in, constantly expecting some manner of nastiness to come springing out at me. Could it be possible that with so many damaged minds in one spot the very building was tainted?

On the other hand, perhaps it was wind brought on by the fish and chips; I had rushed them a bit.

Each time we came to a landing we moved carefully, checking through the glass of the exit doors to make sure we were alone. On the third floor I caught a glimpse of an orderly on his rounds. I just noticed his white back before he vanished through another set of double doors. With any luck he had started at the top of the building and was working his way down, perhaps hoping to finish off in the canteen with a flask of coffee and a packed lunch. If that was the case we were unlikely to cross paths again and all was well.

If he was working his way up then I looked forward to running away from him later.

As it was I needn't have worried. The top floor had staff of its own. The exit door of the staircase led to a corridor that ran towards the front of the building, then, beyond another set of fire doors, it opened out into a large central atrium surrounded by numbered 'cells'. The main staircase opened into the middle of the atrium and, just behind it, a uniformed orderly sat at a desk perusing a glossy skin magazine by the light of his desk lamp. Perhaps he was studying biology? If so it was nice to see him take such pleasure in his work.

"Damn," hissed Dallion. "This isn't going to work is it? To sneak past him is one thing but to rummage around in the same room, unlock one of the doors and then spend a few minutes chatting to a highly emotional child without expecting him to bat an eyelid is perhaps pushing our luck a little."

The orderly turned his magazine around to better appreciate a centre spread and, dear God, I wished I could have seen both of his hands.

"Might work," I said.

Dallion turned his back to the door and closed his eyes.

"Let me just think for a minute." He was silent for a few seconds, brow furrowed. Sandra and I exchanged slightly nervous glances and did our best to forget that we were waiting patiently in a lunatic asylum where we could get caught at any minute.

Slowly he opened one eye and smiled.

"What the hell, it's worth a try."

With that he turned, threw the doors open with both hands and marched towards the orderly.

"It's alright, the mackerel's an oily fish but it's very good for the brain."

The orderly was so startled he nearly fell off his chair, the magazine falling from his hands as he stared at Dallion marching towards him.

Sandra and I jogged behind in an attempt to keep up.

Dallion leaned on the desk, nose to nose with the orderly, talking all the while.

"Think about that now. *Think* about it. An ocean bed filled with a hundredfold mackerel, multiplying over and over two plus two equals eight times thirty-six second cousin twice removed. Who need's the hassle on birthdays? How tall are you? What colour are my eyes?" Dallion swept his fingers across the guard's face, no more than an inch away from his eyes, right to left. "Do you ever get the impression that winter's getting shorter every year? Falling leaves? Falling sun? Falling in love? How many weeks make five? *Go to sleep.*"

With that the guard's eyes rolled upwards and, ever so gently, he slumped forward onto the desk and fell fast asleep.

Dallion grabbed a ledger off the desk and began to pace around the room, checking off the names with the numbers on the doors.

"How on earth did you so that?" I asked, trying to stick by his side.

"Simple bit of linguistic programming. Bombard the brain with more information than it can cope with, throw it into a state of utter panic and confusion and then offer it an escape route; a suggestible person will take that option and wink out for a bit. We won't have long though, five, ten minutes maybe. Aha!"

I tried to peer past him through the glass window of the door he had stopped in front of but it was far too dark for my eyes. By the fact that he was already rummaging in the keyhole with his lock pick I assumed that he had found Jessica's room.

Indeed, once he had opened the door and allowed

some light in I could see her sat on the metal frame bed, a thin woollen blanket wrapped around her shoulders. I stepped forward, looking into her frightened eyes, trying to find the girl I had known before she had disappeared. She looked the same but, forgive me, there was no one in there I recognised.

Suddenly Dallion gave a small cry and put his fingers to his temples.

"What is it?" asked Sandra, putting her hands on his shoulders. He flinched and turned away staggering back out into the atrium.

"Curious...now where did all that come from?" he muttered, moving towards the other side of the atrium. I looked around but, for the life of me, I had no idea what he was referring to. "Happy birthday, Derren," he added, pointing at the room opposite us.

He walked towards it, humming a tune I vaguely recognised, placed his hand on the wood of the door then turned to face me and sang, "*Can I buy your Magic Bus?*" before dropping to the floor. Just crumpled, face first with a grunt as the air was knocked from his body.

With a nervous glance towards Jessica who still sat unmoving on her bed, I ran across to him and turned him on his back. His face was utterly flat, sagging without any emotion; his eyes staring up at the ceiling, though there was little in them to see.

I glanced at the room he had been pointing at. What was in there that had caused him to react so strongly? There was nothing to tell me, nothing discernible in the darkness beyond the glass window. Just the number on the door.

Thirty-Three.

SIX

Like most bastards Gravestown was born while the father was elsewhere.

Scrabbling into life on its own insignificant wedge of dreary coastline with as much real hope of a bright future as a retarded orphan, the odds were against it before the first echoes of its birth trauma had faded.

Hopes had been high; it was to be a place of commerce and affluence, a place of quiet reflection, beauty and tranquillity; a place where all who visited would dream of being able to remain there in perpetuity.

Within half a century it was banging out its 'beauty' with all the pride and respect of a cheap whore on a back street trying to make that month's rent.

The plans were traditional enough, pier and promenade leading back to a small grid of streets lined with shops and hostelries to cater to the illustrious visitors it hoped to attract. A sizeable park and rose garden was plotted for one end of the promenade while a bandstand and solarium would stand proud at the other. When the money dried up and the attention waned the park remained plain and the bandstand jerry rigged. No one cared anymore; the town was beginning to live up to its name. The original, rather egocentric nomenclature of Walgravestown became Gravestown through repetition and carelessness; give it another few decades of consonantal shift and Gravestone will be the name on all the signs (although the wit of many a spray painting youth will beat it by a good few years).

All of which is not to say that the town was a complete failure, just that the benchmark had to be shifted a little; a microwave meal may not bear scrutiny next to a cordon bleu plate but it'll still fill your gut. Money changed hands, good times were had and many people filled the houses that fell back from the centre wave after wave.

For a while at least…

It was the sound that distracted Karen from washing her hands.

High and insistent, like the squeal of a rodent. It took her some time to locate it as the spinning wheel of the air vent in her kitchen window, whipped into a frenzy by the building storm outside. Round and round it went, frantic, urgent, incessant. She watched it for a while before a growing thirst drew her to the kettle and kitchen tap.

She stabbed at the kettle with the carving knife she hadn't been aware of carrying, paused for a moment, confused, then put the knife down and picked the kettle up safely to fill it with water. It nearly slipped in her grip; so slick were her palms with blood. She gripped the handle tighter, filled it from the running tap and then placed the kettle on the stove.

Curious, she thought, as she glanced at her hands. Now where did all that come from?

It slipped her mind for a moment as she lit the gas and listened to the reassuring rush of the blue flame. Then she noticed the continuing flow of water from the tap and turned to shut it off, balking for a moment at the red smears all over the handle. What a mess. She picked up a cloth to wipe it away, pausing as she saw the blood all over her hands again. Tutting to herself she rubbed her hands under the cold water, watching the congealing liquid drip and dilute as it flowed down the plughole. That too was distracting for a few minutes, watching the water become clearer and clearer as the blood washed away. Hadn't she heard that water flowed in the opposite direction in Australia? Anti-clockwise. What would they think of next?

The kettle was beginning to whistle so she turned off the tap, wiping it carefully with the cloth, and returned to making a drink.

She turned off the gas, reached for a tea bag and cup, noticed the bloodstained knife on the worktop and flinched away. What was that doing there? Its blade was large and very sharp, ideal for a Sunday roast, but you did have to be careful; she had nicked herself a couple of times on it over the years, usually when she had been rushing to get dinner ready for Lucas on his return from the pub. Blood had been drawn certainly but never in those quantities. She checked her hands for cuts but found none.

Curious, she thought, as she stared at the blood on the blade. Now where did all that come from?

It couldn't stay there, what if one of the kids found it? They could hurt themselves.

The kids.

Panicking, she picked up the knife, ran out into the hall and up the stairs to the nursery. Well, they called it a nursery but there were few toys, just a pair of cots, hand me downs and the sort of cheap stuffed nonsenses that she could afford with the change Lucas gave her from his beer money. They always said that they would make it nicer one day. Decorate it a little, maybe even a mobile to hang over the cots, she'd seen a lovely one, a moon and stars. She was sure they would like it. Little David was always so curious, reaching for everything he didn't understand, and Susan liked bright things. Shiny, sparkly things, always cooing and chuckling at the necklace Karen wore, as it swung to and fro from her neck; at the bunch of keys she dangled over the cot sometimes; at the spangle sharp blade of the carving knife she always used for the Sunday roast. Giggling and burbling, reaching for it with her soft stubbly little fingers.

Curious, she thought, as her eyes followed the arc sprays of blood that spattered the walls of the nursery. Now where did all that come from?

My goodness but she was thirsty, she'd kill for a cup of tea. As she turned to leave she caught her reflection in the mirror hung on the facing wall. Her dress was ruined. Blood on her chest, blood on her face, blood in her hair. She brushed a stray length away from her face. Lucas wouldn't be too happy to catch her looking like that; Lucas liked things just so.

There was a rattle from the front door. Dear Lord, here he was, home already. He'd want a supper, what had she been thinking dawdling like this? She had nothing prepared.

She ran out of the nursery, steadying herself on the

doorframe as her heel slipped slightly in a wet patch on the carpet, and ran downstairs. She reached the foot of the stairs as the door opened and Lucas stumbled in, yanking awkwardly at his keys to rescue them from the lock. He looked up and dropped his jaw in shock at the sight of the crazed woman running toward him. Karen laughed pleasantly and shoved the carving knife she was still holding straight into his open mouth where it tore his tongue in two before puncturing the top of his windpipe and scraping to a halt across the bone in his neck. He fell back, knocking the door closed with the weight of his body. Pushing himself upright, he spiralled around, a loud wet click coming from his mouth as he involuntarily tried to swallow.

Karen skipped into the kitchen, glad that Lucas didn't seem to be angry with her for not having food ready. Behind her she could hear the high-pitched whistling noises as he struggled to breathe. It confused her for a moment before she glanced at the spinning plastic air vent in the window and remembered. Noticing the kettle on the stove she wondered if he might want a cup of tea with his supper. She picked it up and took it to him in the hall.

She hit him first to the side of the head, splashing boiling water across the flock paper behind him, then once to his stomach and finally square into his face where it hammered the knife deeper. He grunted, coughed a spray of blood into her face and slowly dropped to his knees. Finally, he toppled forward and, as his face hit the carpet, there was another gentle crunch as the point of the knife slid further still, the point erupting from the nape of his neck.

She wiped at her face with her hands, trying to clear the blood from her eyes. She was covered; she really should try and clean herself up. Lucas wouldn't be too happy to catch her looking like this; Lucas liked things just so.

It was the sound that distracted Karen from washing her hands. High and insistent, like the squeal of a rodent. It took her some time to locate it as the spinning wheel of the air vent in her kitchen window, whipped into a frenzy by the building storm outside. Round and round it went, frantic, urgent, incessant. She caught sight of her reflection in the window. Dishevelled and covered in the blood of her family.

Curious, she thought, as she began to cry. Now where did all that come from?

-6.3-

The inherent problem with having a 'kiss me quick' attitude is, of course, that people tend to label you something of a tart.

And, as a knee-jerk response, you can't really blame them. Gravestown set great store in its bright and breezy attitude, in its gaudy spectacle and cheap ale. Arnold Newman, still in firm possession of his chain of mayoral office and many years from stumbling over a child's severed foot on the beach, once had the bravado to go on record as saying "There are more thrills in Gravestown than there are fleas on a Tinker's trousers". It was an unfortunate comment and one he would take a while to live down, however many times he insisted that it was taken out of context (a shallow defence, even if one assumes there could be a context in which Tinker's trousers would sound apposite). It was also something of a lie, or in the spirit of fairness, exaggeration. True it would depend on your definition of thrill, but there was little in Gravestown to which the word could universally be applied. Yes, there was a funfair during the summer months, a temporary pitch arranged around the bandstand that was filled by the *Bertucci Travelling Carnival!* (The rather excitable brainchild of two Glaswegian brothers whose only link to Italy was that their father had shot some of its residents during the war), but even then the rides were, for the most part, sedate affairs. Little more than a selection of child friendly 'turns' as mutually agreed by the town council and the Brothers Bertucci (neé MacGregor) after a group of holidaymakers from Wolverhampton had lost a collective eight front teeth during a moment of abandon concerning the speed control on the part of the Waltzers operator. The ultimate upshot of this being the realisation that: there are only so many times an adult can be ferried around a circular track in a fibre glass mock up of a racing car before the Tinker's trousers sound more fun.

Four penny arcades were dotted along the front, but again, throwing good money after bad in a desperate attempt to win a stuffed toy elephant has a time limit as far as entertainment goes. Nor did it take even the most novice of gamblers long to realise that all of the fruit machines had been cannily adjusted to the 'rape the customer blind' setting as the amount of times they paid out could be seen as proportionate to the amount of Tuesdays in any given week.

There was the pier of course, but beyond the ranks of shuffling perverts pumping the small fixed telescopes with pennies on the hunt for magnified cleavage and a selection of display boards giving the (selective) history of the town there was little else to occupy you.

Once these opportunities for a wild time were sampled there was little to do except rot your guts with ice cream and candyfloss and stand behind the chipped wooden cut-out on the pier to have your photo taken looking like a fat bastard in an Edwardian bathing suit.

All of which had its devotees of course, these were simpler times and the populace was used to 'making do'. Yet, while other seaside towns expanded over the years, stealing bright shiny ideas from America and boosting their market, Gravestown stayed pretty much as it was. It made money, but not much. Achieving that desperate air of a terminal patient maintaining a holding pattern, their past faculties becoming ever more diluted, slowly but surely waiting for death.

-6.4-

If the windows are truly the 'eyes' of a building, then the Bargainrite Bonanza didn't see the Molotov cocktail coming as it already been blinded by a well aimed hail of bricks.

The fire lashed across aisles four and five (homeware and cleaning products) and sent a tongue whipping against the back wall where it took hold of a poster advertising two for one on Daz washing powder.

The boys took their seats on the bonnets of the cars parked outside and settled back with a packet of stolen cigarettes.

There were five of them in total: Derren Bright, Luke Handsworthy, Peter Morris (although his friends called him 'Tonto' due to his prodigious buck teeth), Mike Fowler and Colin Reilly (son of Tony Reilly, the pier's medical officer and brief media darling after he'd been the one to bundle the foot up and out of harm's way a few weeks back). It was Derren's birthday, which placed him a clear four months older than the rest.

He was thirteen.

They were waiting by the burning shop for a reason; not only did they want to watch their handiwork grow, they wanted to see what would happen when the fire reached the owner's flat. They were pretty sure that the only way out was via the passage and stairs behind the shop counter, had seen old Brian Greene come and go that way frequently when they had queued to buy sweets from his wife, Eileen, who was commonly behind the till.

He was a little unsteady on his legs these days, the stick he'd reserved for when the weather was damp or there was ice on the paths had been a permanent fixture over the last couple of months. They hadn't expected him to come running at the sound of breaking glass therefore, and there was no way Eileen would be the first face at the strip curtain that led out back, there were mice with braver temperaments. Taking all of this into consideration they had estimated a response time of nearly two minutes, thirty seconds for the shock, another forty or so for the pulling on of a dressing gown and retrieval of his stick, same again for the cautious negotiation of the stairs. It might be even more if he paused to call the police rather than order his wife to do it. Not that it would achieve anything, they'd cut the phone cables along the street before they'd raised their first stone, something Mike had suggested after remembering an episode of Dragnet from a few weeks before.

The flames were getting thoroughly entrenched on the opposite side of the shop to the exit. They hoped the fire wasn't going to get too advanced before Brian made an appearance, that would take all of the fun out of it, there was still a sizeable pile of broken bricks on the pavement in front of them and they were there to be used.

Luke checked his watch; the old man had had his two minutes. As one they shuffled off the bonnets and began to select their favourite weapons. Colin selected according to size, for Peter sharpness was the key.

The strip curtain parted briefly, they heard the old man shout to his wife and, after another few seconds they both made their way onto the shop floor. Bonus. The boys allowed them to clear the passage by a few feet, moving quickly but cautiously towards the front door and broken windows, it would be a tactical error on their part if the couple had darted back out of sight as soon as they realised the boys were still there.

Derren (who had selected a mid-sized brick fragment, shaped bizarrely, he thought, like a poodle's head) went first.

It was his birthday after all...

-6.5-

However proficient they were with balloon animals, you wouldn't ask a clown to fit your bathroom.

And therein lay Gravestown's problem: It did what it did but no more. There was no great business, no industry, nothing to fall back on. It was inevitable therefore that should the bottom fall out of its tourist market there would be no keeping the town afloat. There were those that commuted elsewhere for their employment of course, and as long as there were a few of them then someone else would be able to make money by keeping them fed and watered. That covered the backs of the shop owners whose trades were aimed as much at the locals as the tourists. Didn't help you much if you earned your crust from hard rock sweets fashioned into amusing shapes though; there are only so many boiled egg or breast shaped fancies a household can legitimately own, even assuming they take the plunge and wipe out their supply by eating them.

New residents of the town looked elsewhere for their income, the dynamics began to shift, Gravestown became less a place you went to, more a place you started from. The bus and train service told the story best, all seats full on the way out, empty on the way in.

Which means, whichever way you cut it, it was going to end in tears one way or another.

-6.6-

Jeremy Ashe had had sex twice since the action on the pier and he was coming to the rather unpleasant conclusion that he wasn't very good at it.

The realisation made him give a dismissive grunt towards the rather sleepy looking Joan and take a stroll along the beach.

After they had given the freak a damn good kicking they had picked up the girls and gone out to walk the streets for a while; hunting for the next thrill, settling for sitting around on the sand when they hadn't found one. Jeremy felt drunk, probably was drunk a little; the gin in his system had vanished after the pier, adrenaline burning it off very quickly, but he'd had a few sips since. Not many mind, because, truth be told, he felt a little sick. Sick and confused. There were three distinct emotions rolling around his hormone-addled brain; fear, guilt and lastly, God help him, *pride*. It was one thing to know that you'd done something wrong, to be aware deep within your gut that you'd crossed a moral line that just shouldn't be crossed.

It was something else again to realise you'd liked it.

There had been a great sense of power, still was, he'd listened to the voice in his head, acted on it, and now the world was a different place because of him. For better or worse was almost immaterial.

He knew it was wrong (Jesus, so wrong), but he had to make a choice: to step back from it, to admit his culpability and take the consequences, or to keep going.

He knew what he should do...

But the voice in his head was still talking and it was getting so hard to think...

Glancing up at the streetlights and the road he saw something coming towards them and all rational thought vanished; vanished to be replaced with something altogether worse: an idea.

He ran towards the road, shouting over his shoulder to the gang behind him, still lolling about on the sand, directionless and functionless without him - and the voice inside him - to light a fire beneath them.

He didn't check to see if they were following, just jumped up on the sea wall and climbed over onto the pavement on the other side. Not even looking to see if there was any traffic, he sprinted across and along to the bus stop where the number 12 was letting out its last customer of the night.

He jumped through the closing door and, even while the driver was trying to say that his route was done, just the short hop to the depot and home to bed, he punched him full in the face. Then again, and again, before the man even had time to react. The fourth was the charm, the driver was old and overweight, trapped in his seat, Jeremy however was young and able to put the full weight of his body behind the blows. There was a crack as his knuckles connected with the bridge of the man's nose, sending shards of bone swimming back into grey matter, a spurt of blood from his nostrils and then he slumped back against the driver's side window.

The pain was beginning to grow in Jeremy's hand but, for now, the adrenaline and the excited screaming in his head held it back. He reached for the catch that would release the barrier between them, flipped it open and pulled the driver from his seat, letting his own dead weight send him toppling to the floor of the bus. He then rolled him with his feet, pushing him out of the door and onto the pavement outside where he landed with a puff of air at the feet of Keith and Dave who had caught up with him by now. Looking out of the front windscreen he could see Ann and Joan on the other side of the road, gazing over in sleepy confusion.

"What are you waiting for?" he shouted. "Hop on

board."

He clambered into the driver's seat and hunted for the ignition, pulling the barrier closed behind him.

Keith and Dave shared a look, laughed and then cheered as the bus engine roared into life. They waved the girls over and they all clambered on board as Jeremy tried to get a feel for the pedals. Suddenly he paused, aware again of the voice in his head, whispering instructions. God bless the King of Mods, he thought, where would I be without him?

"Where are we going?" asked Joan as she fell into one of the seats. Jeremy chuckled, pulled out onto the road and slammed down the accelerator.

"Wherever the fuck we want darling, this is the Magic Bus, last stop: Cliff Richard's front lawn."

-6.7-

All of which begs the question: at what point would it be acceptable to commit euthanasia on a town?

Even acknowledging the inherent difficulty in carrying out the mercy killing we would have to say the patient was really starting to beg for it. There was scant hope for long-term survival and little genuine pleasure of life left in its streets. Wouldn't it be the kindest thing in the long run?

Sadly it's not our choice to make, besides if we were to extend the analogy; continue in our anthropomorphosis of town to living being, it seemed to be doing a rather good job of it itself. Much more of this sort of behaviour and it would certainly burn up in an act of self-destruction in very little time at all. Or perhaps it would survive only to be pulled up in front of the courts, maybe even plead diminished responsibility? For there can be little question as the night unfolded, as its streets and houses erupted in violence and chaos, as its populace looked up at the moon outside its window and began to feel an itch deep inside.

Gravestown had become completely and utterly insane

SEVEN

The Adventures of Gregory Ashe: Episode Thirteen – Black Peril of Doom

To recap then:

Your gallant adventurer (that would be me for the slow on the uptake) seems to have found himself breaking into a lunatic asylum accompanied by a mysterious street magician called Dallion and a sometime gypsy and tarot master Rosa Carlotta (real name: Sandra Duckworth – cynical chain smoker and foul mouth). All concerned decided on this rather foolhardy course of action in an attempt to break one of the patients free; a young girl who, after being kidnapped by mystical forces unknown, reappeared and proceeded to try and kill her parents. Many would deem this foolish, including yours truly in hindsight, having realised that being trapped on the top floor of said asylum with an unconscious orderly and an equally unconscious street magician (who had the singular bad timing to 'go for a burton' mid-way through the breakout) is not something he had anticipated. The Magician dazzled all with this mind-blowing piece of planning right after pointing at another room on the same level, number Thirty-Three. Luckily Sandra had a cunning plan:

"Throw the useless sod out of the closest window, we'll pick him up on the way out!"

Join us next week when we feature the thrilling conclusion of our tale in: *Episode Fourteen: 'Gregory Hunts for the Librium'.*

-7.2-

"That's about as constructive as giving a paraplegic roller skates for his birthday!"

I shouted, trying to shake Dallion awake.

"Probably just as fun too!" Sandra began pacing. "What are we going to do, for God's sake? We can't just stay here!"

"I don't know, now calm down and go and check on Jessica."

"Oh God..." Sandra ran back to the room we had just opened, having clearly forgotten about the girl in her panic.

Not that I could blame her for panicking. God, *I* felt like panicking; felt like locking myself in one of these rooms (or cells, they looked and felt more like cells) and waiting patiently for the lobotomy. But still, if I'm truthful there was more than a little... I can hardly believe I'm admitting it but... *excitement* to all this. Beating the humdrum that had been suffocating me before, living just the sort of adventure that every kid wants to find round the corner, even when they know that it'll end up being the same old same old. Yes, so I was trapped in a lunatic asylum, surrounded by the damaged and deranged. Yes, we had just opened the door on a girl who was incarcerated here due to the fact that she attempted to mindlessly slaughter her parents. Yes, I had just sent a panicking Sandra to go and comfort this potential murderer.

Oh... What an *idiot*...

Sandra gave a short yell and, glancing up, I saw Jessica running towards me, eyes wild, small fingers spread like claws, eager to do some damage.

"Somebody sack the babysitter." Dallion's voice startled me almost as much as the sight of a young girl I had once known but clearly didn't know any longer.

He sat bolt upright, grabbed at Jessica and swung her down into his arms, like a lover in an old movie, Gone with the Wind, Brief Encounter, something along those lines. He swept his hand gently across her face and shushed her like a baby. She closed her eyes and fell limp.

Sandra came out of Jessica's cell, rubbing at her left eye.

"Little git shoved her thumb in my face, bit my hand and did a runner."

"You obviously have a way with children," Dallion murmured, still stroking at Jessica's hair. He settled Jessica, now clearly asleep, onto the floor and stood up.

"What happened to you?" I asked.

"I don't really know." He looked around him, eyes falling on the door to Thirty-Three again. "There's something in the air, like the wind changing on a mental level. I'm rather sensitive in many ways, the sudden... *psychic* surge knocked me for six a little."

He walked over to the door and laid his palm on its surface.

"It's all kicking off out there, in the town, in the people. Part of that, a *reflection* of that seemed to come out of here."

He turned to look at the orderly who was, amazingly, still out for the count.

"We've got to get whoever it is in there out."

"Oh come on!" Sandra hissed. "That can't be sensible, can it? Haven't we got enough on our hands with The Bad Seed here?" She gestured at Jessica and I felt myself squirm at the reddening around her eye; a fraction to the left and she could have lost it.

"She'll be okay for awhile, I've put her in a low state, she shouldn't be able to do much more than blink for an hour or two. I know it's a risk but whoever's in that room is connected to all of this in a vital way. We need to know how, why and whether they hold any kind of key to stopping it."

"Well, you're going in first," Sandra sighed, and went back to massaging her eye.

"Fair enough," he said and reached into his pocket for the lock pick.

I moved over to his shoulder, as concerned as Sandra as to what may lie on the other side of the door but as eager as Dallion to find some answers to it all.

The lock clicked and he gently turned the handle.

-7.3-

Number 33 screamed as the light from the hallway fell on her.

It was brief and muted by a hand in front of her mouth but I looked to the sleeping orderly nonetheless, he rolled a little on the desk and I was convinced he was waking. Then a soft snore came from between his lips and I breathed again. Sandra tiptoed over to keep an eye on him.

I turned back to the cell and looked closely at the woman inside. I mistook her for elderly at first; the streaks of white in her hair caught within the neon light from the hallway were immediately striking. But, on closer inspection, you could see that her face was unlined, soft, the face of a young woman. Her hair was long and, with the exception of those white streaks, very dark, which is why it had almost vanished in the partial shadow leaving only the white to be seen. She held her blanket up to her chest, huddled protectively like Jessica, but still you could tell that she was dreadfully thin, her forearms appearing little more than bones.

"I'm sorry," she whispered, as if fearful of who might be listening, "it was the light, I thought it was... something else."

"You thought it was what?" asked Dallion, whispering in the same soft tone as he slowly moved towards her bed.

She looked at him, fearful in one moment then almost mocking in the next, as if he was being stupid, it was the face you would give to a particularly dense child.

"Don't be silly."

"Of course, sorry." Dallion looked towards me and raised an eyebrow. "But I really don't know what you mean."

The look of fear passed across her face again and I wondered whether it might be foolish to press the point for now.

"It doesn't matter though, does it?" I said, putting what I hoped was enough inflection in my voice to convey my point to Dallion.

He looked to me again and nodded gently.

"Of course it doesn't," he smiled. "Just me being thick again. I really am dreadfully slow at times, you mustn't mind me."

"That's alright," she said and patted him on the hand. "Not all of us can be clever, I knew as much when I first saw you."

I chuckled to watch him squirm.

"Well... yes, is it that obvious?"

"Don't worry, I'll look after you." She smiled lovingly at him, like a mother to a child. "Are we going away from here?"

"Would you like that?"

"A trip would be nice, I can show you lots of things, maybe even teach you a little." She stood up and walked past me into the hallway. Dallion dashed to follow, whispering in my ear as he passed.

"Fancy thinking I'm stupid, she *must* be insane."

"Whatever you say," I grinned and, closing the door, followed them.

Sandra was still stood by the orderly but she came dashing over as soon as she saw the new arrival.

"Oh, we're letting them all out, are we? Fair enough, I'm sure they're all lovely people really, just misunderstood."

Thirty-Three smiled at her and shook her head.

"Don't be silly, you wouldn't want to let these people out."

"Why?" asked Dallion.

"They're completely mad."

"They're not the only ones," said Sandra after a pause, giving Dallion a pointed stare.

"Yes... well perhaps we'd better be on our way. Constable Dibble over there could wake up at any moment." He picked Jessica up carefully and put her over his shoulder in a fireman's lift. "We can discuss all this somewhere a little more private."

He strolled over towards the doors where we'd come in. Suddenly he spun around and dashed back towards us.

"The other orderly's coming! Come on, main stairs!"

I quickly dashed to Jessica's cell and pulled the door closed before running after them down the main stairway. There was no point in letting the orderly know something was amiss the minute he came in. With any luck we'd be out of here before anyone realised they were a couple of patients light.

As I turned around the first bend in the stairs I heard the double doors swing open.

"Dear God... wake up you lazy sod!" a voice shouted; there was a startled grunt from the desk, and then I was gone.

Although I had only taken a few seconds to close the door the rest of the group were almost a full floor ahead of me, Dallion moving in long loping strides despite the extra weight of the child on his back. I moved as quickly and quietly as I could to catch up, noticing Dallion dart onto the third floor. Thankfully he drew the group to a halt just off the staircase allowing me to join them.

"This is exciting!" said Thirty-Three, grinning like a schoolgirl on an outing.

"Isn't it?" replied Dallion, disturbingly free of sarcasm. "If we cut across this floor we should get to the rear stairway and be in a better position to sneak out the back."

He dashed through a pair of double doors, Thirty-Three skipping behind him. Sandra held her hand across my chest for a moment.

"Keep an eye on that one, Gregory, I don't trust her for a minute."

"She seems fine."

"That's all very well but remember what Dallion said about the inmates on the top floor, if he was right then there was a probably a very good reason why she was kept apart from the others. Just stay on your guard." She had a very good point.

We passed through another set of double doors and then along a cell lined corridor that turned at a sharp right angle before another length of corridor led to the rear stairway at its far end.

Dallion had paused in front of the door to the stairs.

"Right, just in case, hang back a second while I check that the coast is clear. I'm fairly certain that a place like this would only operate on a couple of night staff..." He stuck his head around the door before pulling it back quickly. "Well, *three* at most." He dashed back the way we'd come leaving Sandra and I looking at one another in slight confusion. Then we heard a gentle cough from the other side of the stairway door and the penny dropped.

We ran like hell to get around the corner and out of sight before the orderly came off the stairs. I heard the door open just as I cleared his line of sight and dashed along the corridor only to bump into Dallion and Thirty-Three again.

"Slight technical hitch," he hissed. "The one from

upstairs is coming this way."

I looked around in panic, we were surrounded and there was no exit, just the doors to the cells.

Oh, but that couldn't be a very good idea...

I looked at Dallion and he smiled,

"Does seem the only option, doesn't it rather?"

He snatched the lock pick from his pocket and began to work on the closest cell. To my left I could hear the sound of the orderly's footsteps, the jangle of keys hanging from his belt. To my right there was the sound of the first set of double doors opening.

"Quickly!" whispered Sandra, a slight edge of hysteria in her voice.

"All the time in the world..." mumbled Dallion as the lock clicked open and he pushed us all in. He swung the door closed, gently slipping the latch into place behind him. He gestured for all of us to keep clear of the glass window in the door, pressing back against the wall.

I looked behind me into the room, it was dark but the light spilling through the glass in the door showed a body lying in the bed, it shifted slightly, turning in its sleep I hoped.

Outside the door we saw the orderly from the stairway walk past, waving to his colleague from upstairs. They started talking just along the corridor from us, not ten feet from the door.

"Come on!" I whispered, looking over to Dallion for suggestions. I couldn't see his face in the shadow but his free arm suddenly appeared in the beam of light from the corridor outside, it was shaking furiously. "Dallion?"

I slipped past the door to his side, grabbing him by the shoulder; he was shaking all over.

"What is it, what's wrong?"

His face fell into the light and I could see that his eyes were closed tight, his teeth clenched. Sandra whispered from the dark beyond him.

"What's going on?"

Barely audible he hissed from between his teeth.

"Like before, but worse, it's all going..."

Suddenly his eyes sprang open just as the body in the bed sat bolt upright.

They both screamed.

I scream, you scream; we all scream for ice cream...

...flashed bizarrely through my head as I realised that it wasn't just Dallion and the stranger whose room we'd broken into that were screaming. All along the corridor cries rang out from the cells. For all I could tell, hands pressed against my ears in the dark, the entire building was screaming its throat raw.

I couldn't hear the orderlies but one clearly ran past the window, maybe on the hunt for assistance, maybe just to get out of here.

Sandra grabbed at Dallion, pulling Jessica from his shoulder before he dropped her.

Thirty-Three stood still in the shadows, unmoving, unknowing.

The resident of the room we were all stood in leapt from the bed and sent me sprawling to the floor under his weight. I could tell now that it was an old man, his bony chest colliding with my face and sending a burst of white lights before my eyes. Dazed but sufficiently afraid to keep some semblance of wits about me I grabbed at his wrists as he aimed for my eyes with his spindly fingers. He was old and wiry but the panic or delusion had lent him extra strength and I struggled to keep his nails away from my face. I felt a rush of guilt as I brought my leg pounding up between his, wincing as he coughed and spat a shocked wad of saliva onto my cheek. Still he held on.

Then a shadow passed behind him and I heard Sandra grunt in exertion as she thrashed down on his head with her shoe. He cried out as she did it again, then once more for good luck until he toppled off me, clutching his head in his hands.

"Let's get out of here!" she shouted, grabbing at Jessica and swinging her rather roughly over her shoulders. She pulled the door open, gave the corridor a quick check, and then ran out of the room.

I shoved Dallion towards the open doorway and, with a slight hint of worry, held my hand out to Thirty-Three.

"Come on, we've got to go."

She looked at me blankly for a moment then smiled and took my hand. We both ran out together.

Dallion was running in front of me, no longer screaming but swaying from side to side as if drunk; it was clearly taking some degree of concentration on his part just to move. For now he was winning the battle, moving steadily after Sandra towards the rear staircase.

It suddenly occurred to me that I should have closed the door and I glanced over my shoulder to see the man who had attacked me shuffle naked from his room and start banging at the other doors along the corridor.

We burst onto the stairway, not really caring if we met anyone by then. It would take some degree of force to keep us in the building with the steady screams of its inhabitants still echoing around the walls; anyone likely to try it would most probably end up with a natty collection of footprints from toe to topknot. As it was the staff were clearly elsewhere, trying to control the situation. We cleared the last three levels at break-neck speed, out onto the ground floor and along the corridor towards the rear of the building.

As we burst through the kitchen and out into the fresh air I wished whoever was left inside luck, sure that it would take greater force than the orderlies possessed to bring the situation under control. The Cliff Tops was in the grip of some kind of fever and if I were an employee I would be inclined to just let nature take its course.

Dallion grabbed me by the shoulder.

"Sorry," he said breathlessly. "That was a little difficult back there."

"It's alright," I said, relieved to see that he appeared more in control again.

He nodded gratefully and dashed to the outside wall where Sandra was waiting.

"I'll jump up first and take Jessica from you."

He vaulted up and, gripping the bricks between his legs, reached down for Jessica.

"Careful with her," said Sandra, straining to lift the girl above her head.

"Of course," he replied, a touch impatiently. He took

hold of her and lowered her partway down the other side of the wall. "Perhaps you'd like to just hop over and take her from me?"

Sandra sighed and beckoned me over to give her a foot up.

"Certainly, just 'hopping over' now."

She put her foot between my laced hands and pulled herself up and over, landing with a graceless 'bollocks!' on the other side.

Dallion straightened up as Sandra relieved him of his charge and beckoned Thirty-Three to join him.

She was looking around in a mixture of excitement and abject terror, like a caged animal ready to bolt at any moment now the gate has been left open.

I offered my hands but she ignored them and continued to amble around the patio frequently looking up at the sky as if in search for birds of prey.

"Please!" I said in desperation. "We have to go."

Suddenly there was a loud crash of breaking glass from above us, Thirty-Three gave a cry of panic and ran straight past me, scrabbling up the wall with her fingers and toes. Dallion grabbed at her before she fell and pulled her up to join him.

I looked up at the window that had broken, a shower of glass raining down around the body of the man that had fallen (or been pushed) through it. Even in the dark I recognised his face as it passed through the beams of light from the building's windows; it was the orderly who had been sat upstairs. He landed on one of the large stone planters, the sound of his back snapping on the filigreed edge audible above the continued cries from the patients inside.

"Now, Gregory!" Dallion shouted as he helped Thirty-Three down to the other side of the wall.

Accepting that there was absolutely nothing I could do for the orderly who lay folded backwards in the flowerbed, face down in the dirt, legs hanging limp by his head, I turned towards the wall and jumped for the top. Dallion's hand gripped me by the back of my shirt and hauled me up to join him.

"It's going to get worse, Gregory," he said quietly enough that the others couldn't hear. "You're going to have to prepare yourself for that, I'm afraid."

"I'm alright."

"No you're not. Neither am I. Nor *should* we be. But we're going to have to carry on regardless."

"I know."

We jumped down to the grass together and he patted me on the back.

"What was that?" asked Sandra, still cradling Jessica in her arms.

Dallion looked at me for a moment before replying.

"Nothing we can do anything about, I'm just glad we got out when we did. Let's get to the car."

She narrowed her eyes, aware that there was something she wasn't being told but obviously deciding that now wasn't the time to push it as she turned around and began to make her way along the ledge towards the front of the building.

Thirty-Three was still looking frightened, her back pressed against the wall. Dallion waved me on and took her hand.

"It's alright," he said quietly. "We're safe now; let's go home, shall we?"

She looked up at him with round inquiring eyes.

"Home?"

"That's right, where we'll be even safer."

She appeared to think for a moment before nodding gently and allowing herself to be led away.

Sandra paused at the front of the building, checking the road for sign of any emergency vehicles or maybe extra staff drafted in to help with the chaos. If either had been called they'd obviously not had time to reach us yet as the road was dark. Shuffling Jessica so she sat more comfortably across her shoulders she ran out to the side of the drive and towards the main road. I followed, like her not caring much if we stayed to the shadows. There would be no threat from behind, they had more pressing matters; as long as the drive ahead remained clear we should be home dry.

I was brought to a sudden halt by the sound of Thirty-Three screaming behind me. I turned around to see her thrashing in Dallion's arms pointing up at the sky. I followed where she was looking but, other than the moon, I saw nothing.

I started back towards them, watching as she

turned to face Dallion, pounding at his arms and chest. Suddenly he dropped his hold and stumbled backwards, heading straight towards the cliff's edge.

I ran quicker, pushing past Thirty-Three and reaching out to grab him.

He looked at me vaguely, his eyes taking on a lost look. Then his heel caught on a small mound and slipped from underneath him. He rolled briefly before tumbling over the edge.

"Dallion!" I screamed, dropping to my belly on the edge of the cliff. Pulling myself forward I could see him just below me, the nails of both hands buried painfully tight into the long grass and rock. I tried to reach out to him, felt my fingers brushing the tense back of his left hand.

"Gregory," he hissed, barely able to phrase the word, straining to hold on.

"Take my hand!" I shouted, knowing full well that I couldn't take his weight if he did but unable not to try.

He looked up at me, his face suddenly becoming calm as his hands lost their grip and he floated backwards into the air.

"Sorry," he said and dropped swiftly down. "*Soft Places!*" his voice shouted up before it cut off abruptly, the last half a syllable replaced by the roar of waves and the sound of lunatics screaming.

EIGHT

There was something in the walls...

...Lucy had been aware of it for some time, lying awake night after night listening to the itch scritch scratch of movement. Her Mummy and Daddy didn't believe her of course, just shook their heads in that irritating way that grown ups did and tucked Brian the bear under the blankets next to her.

Good old Brian, a noble if scruffy old bear whose glass bead eyes twinkled with a humour that often made Lucy chuckle. When you turned the key in his spine his belly filled with jangles, 'Teddy Bears Picnic' in a small bell serenade. She played it often, especially when the walls were noisy; sometimes it made them shut up.

Every now and then, when the walls were particularly loud, Lucy had called Mummy and Daddy into the room. Of course they always went quiet as soon as they stepped through the door.

Well, except for tonight of course... but she didn't want to think about that right now.

(Especially not that mess on the wallpaper, or the arm jutting out, fingers clenching at first then twisted and still. Daddy's arm.)

No... best to forget about all that. She stroked Brian's head and sang about happy things, quietly though... no sense in asking for trouble.

The walls began to grumble.

Lucy pulled the blankets over her head and continued to sing, stroking and tugging hard at Brian's fur.

The bed began to shake...

-8.2-

"Pink, corner pocket!"

Jeremy hit the old woman with the front left bumper and laughed like a loon as she flew backwards into the rear windscreen of a parked car. The bus was surprisingly easy to drive (or maybe it was just the whispered voice in his ear telling him what to do every step of the way) and he was having a wonderful time swinging it fast round the tight corners of the town. He thrashed it along the straights, occasionally clipping a parked car or terrified pedestrian just for larks. If nothing else it gave them something to do while waiting for a better idea.

Holding pattern, that's what it was. He couldn't tell you how he knew that but there was no doubt in his mind that something big was on its way. The sort of thing you just don't walk away from.

Which suited him just fine, thank you very much.

In the distance he could see a couple running down the street hand in hand. How sweet.

He stamped his foot down hard and swung the steering wheel with a grin.

-8.3-

Were it not for the trail of gull shit down his left cheek, Joshua Walgrave would still cut something of a dash.

But then the statue was a popular spot for people polishing off their fish and chips - the base was encircled by a wooden slat bench and was no more than two hundred yards from 'Giuseppe's', the most popular frying house in town - and it takes a foolish scavenger indeed not to earmark such locations as being good for a few easy scraps.

At night it took on a different atmosphere, being popular amongst young couples as a place to sit and canoodle a little (give it twenty years and the couples would get younger and the canoodling much heavier), the sea was loud and the view was good; sit at the right angle and you could almost forget that the town was a bit of a dump.

Tonight it was a return visit for Tom Wilkie and the delectable Tina Bosworth. They'd been coming here every Tuesday for nigh on six weeks. Every night was the same; Tom would laugh too much and too loud while Tina sighed and wondered about giving up on the damn man to ever make his move. He was sweet enough, at least in the 'beggars can't be choosers' world of Gravestown, where if the men weren't married they were either too drunk or too repulsive to ever become so. Dear Lord, he was boring though. Whenever she went out with him she could be sure of nothing more than soporific conversation - about boats usually, Tom had a thing about boats, it was the only thing she'd ever seen him get excited about - and a long walk home (he didn't own a car and, unless Ford started manufacturing a model with a topsail and poop deck, was unlikely to ever do so).

To his credit he would always pay for supper and notice if she'd had her hair done but sometimes - most especially when sat on the front row of the Picture House in town wishing he'd put his arm around her - she would find herself wondering whether there couldn't be a bit more to life. Anything really...

Why couldn't something exciting ever happen?

There was a terrible deep roar of bending metal and Tom and Tina leapt off the bench as, behind them, the statue of Joshua Walgrave began to move.

It snatched at the seagull that had been sat on its shoulder, gripping it firm in its bronze fist before opening its cold mouth and forcing the bird into the toothless hole. The metal lips clamped shut with a solitary feather jutting out.

"Well," said Tom. "There's something you don't see everyday."

The statue turned to look at them and its arm reached out...

-8.4-

...out towards the sea.

A tear fell from Walgrave's cold cold eye and, for a moment, it occurred to him that it was probably the first to fall since it had happened. Now that just couldn't be natural, could it? But then naturalism was a notion that had been fading for some time. Each day was an unreal slurry of hours, hours and minutes with no way to mark them.

Until now of course, he thought, glancing down at the object in the sand.

What was another impossibility when one's life was made up of such things?

He stooped down to pick up his pocket watch, the watch he had used to weight the coffin down, the watch that he had given away to the sea many weeks ago, the watch that couldn't possibly be lying here now ticking away beneath the scream of gulls.

He looked into its polished face and hunted for answers; there were none.

Looking out across the tides again he became aware of more, something out there, something watching. His eyes couldn't catch it but then where was the mystery in that? After all...

-8.5-

Just because you can't see something doesn't mean it's not there.

Lucy may have been a couple of months off her sixth birthday but she already knew that much. Besides, even with the blanket over her head she could still hear the noises, the scratching, crunching, grinding, and the bed *was* rocking like a ship in a storm. At this point *not* seeing didn't make matters any less scary.

She leaped off the bed, pulling Brian with her, and pressed herself against the closed door to her room. The bed stopped moving, lying at an angle across the floor.

She held Brian in front of her like a charm. As an afterthought she gave the key in his back a few twists and the tinny bells began to play...

"If you go down to the woods today..."

The wall began to move, to ripple.

In a roar of shattering masonry a crack widened across the horizontal of the wall, just as it had before, when Mummy and Daddy...

When it *took* them.

Daddy's arm fell to the floor, released from the grip of the bricks. There was nothing on the end of it, the rest of him was gone. Eaten. Eaten by the thing in the wall.

By the thing that *was* the wall.

The crack widened and smiled its cracked brick smile.

"You're sure of a big surprise..."

The wall surged forward, mouth open wide and hungry.

Lucy screamed.

The music stopped.

The rest was blood and brick dust...

NINE

The notion of death is a bigger thing than death itself.

Death is small, instant, the difference between a firm grip and a fistful of air. Death is the *bringer* of consequence, more often the instigator of hardship rather than hardship itself. This is an unpleasant thing to accept, an attitude riddled with guilt and self-questioning. It's also utterly true.

Had I known him long enough to call him a friend? No, not really, although 'in the kingdom of the blind the one eyed man is king'... my social circle was hardly wide. After Sandra - and that was little more than puppy love, I'll admit to that - the next on my list of friends was probably next door's dog. Frankly, any one of the writers on my bookshelves would beat them both hands down; I certainly spent more time with them.

Dallion was dead.

There really wasn't much doubt about that, miraculous he may be but it would take more than temporal trickery and prodigious sleight of hand to negotiate a fall like that.

Right now I felt nothing. Nothing except the beginnings of fear and a selfish surge of bitterness; how on earth were we to survive without him?

"Come on!" Sandra shouted, a wild look on her face. For all her swagger she was a hair's breadth from snapping, it was taking every ounce of self determination to keep it together for long enough to get us all out of there.

"The moon took him," said Number Thirty-Three, a serene look on her pale face. "It takes us all in the end."

She nodded and walked after Sandra who had begun to run towards the car.

I paused for a minute, trying to feel grief, then ran after them.

"Soft Places."

That's what he'd said. Face pressed against the car window as we drove back to town, Number Thirty-Three occasionally cooing or chuckling at the world we drove past, the expression rolled over and over in my mind. As final words they were bizarre to say the least, which meant they were probably important.

'Soft Places'.

God help me, but I had no idea what he'd meant.

As we descended into town it was immediately obvious something had happened in the short time we'd been away. When you grow up in a place you become attuned to its vibrations, its *essence*. The atmosphere was wrong, we could tell as much from inside the car. It wasn't a war zone, there were no burning buildings or bomb craters, but once you paid attention the cracks began to show: smashed windows, dented cars, and, pulling onto the main street, a couple of bodies - clearly dead - crumpled in the gutter.

Gravestown was beginning to self-destruct.

"What the bloody hell's been going on here?" Sandra whispered, pulling over to the side of the road.

I flinched as she opened the driver's door and dashed over to one of the fallen bodies. It was in the air, you could *smell* it.

"We shouldn't hang around," I said, looking up and down the street for signs of trouble. Somewhere in the distance I heard the sound of a heavy engine - a lorry or bus perhaps - over revving.

Sandra turned the body over; it was Dilys McKenzie, owner of the Second Chance Dress Agency next door to the Town Hall, although the contorted snarl on her face made it clear that she wouldn't be as lucky as the second hand dresses and skirts she filled her rails with. There would be no extra lease of life for Dilys.

"Dear God," Sandra muttered, turning the body over.

"God's away," Number Thirty-Three sang. She'd got out of the car behind us and was skipping along the pavement looking in windows. "God's away, God's away on business."

God.

("Time gets soft in these places.")

Dallion's voice. Memory.

"Come on, Sandra!" I shouted, getting back into the car. "We've got to get back to the house."

-9.3-

"This is too much, you know that?"

Sandra was slipping; I could hear it in her voice, see it in her shaking hands as she tried to pull a cigarette out of its pack. "I mean, look at us, a charlatan and a child. We should be loading up the car and making for the hills."

We'd arrived back at the house and I'd tried to explain to her about the journey Dallion and I had made from his room upstairs.

She wasn't coping with it very well.

I understood how she felt; Dallion had been the accelerant, the force that had kept us moving quick enough to ignore the situation. With him gone it all seemed ludicrous. Perhaps, as he'd suggested before, he had manipulated us into being his little private army, kept our thoughts away from the danger and surrealism of it all. She was right, it seemed nonsensical, unreasonable, beyond us completely. Still, I wanted to keep going, though through an arrogant sense of my own self worth or the inability to let go I couldn't say. One thing I did know, though, is that we might not be quite as alone as she thought.

"Don't worry about it, Sandra. You've got to look after Number Thirty-Three and Jessica; they need you. Leave this bit to me. I know what I'm doing."

Which was, of course, a blatant lie but she didn't need to know that. All she needed was something more down to earth to worry about - maternal instinct, a natural protectiveness, whatever... it was the only thing that had kept her going this far and I hoped it had enough potency to hold her together for a few more hours yet.

Even as I said it I could hear the manipulation in my own voice, playing her just as Dallion had played us from that first moment on the beach.

And, damn, but it felt *right*.

I dashed up to Dallion's room and searched for the bottle of whiskey. It was lying propped up against a few books on tarot and a large biography of Errol Flynn. I sat cross-legged on the floor and, raising a quick toast to Errol, took a large slug. I stroked the stone about my neck and hoped that I could repeat the experience of a few hours before. We needed a little help from God.

A god called Charlie.

I closed my eyes and tried to catch a taste of that dry desert air, that black ash landscape, that shadow sky.

Whether it was because the doorway was still partly open or I genuinely had some ability I couldn't say, but after two more mouthfuls of whiskey and a head full of sheer bloody desperation I felt the carpet slip away from beneath me. A breeze began to ripple the curtains sending a chill across my sweating forehead.

Heartbeat slowed... a dizzy feeling of vertigo... slippery shiver of passing... and I was...

-9.4-

...Out.

Tumbling down the dune-like mound of black ash. I stopped/am stopping my fall with my hands and struggled/am struggling to my feet. Elsewhere. Everywhen.

It was different to before, not as controlled. Time running wild. The land appeared in flux, constantly shifting in and out of focus. Above me in the dark absence that passed for a sky I heard - or maybe felt - something turn on leathery wings and hunt the landscape for prey.

(Temporal meat.)

I looked about, trying to find familiarity, trying to recognise. I ran, hands outstretched, searching for the way out/ way in.

Beginning to panic I shouted (*I'm screaming*) and barely sensed the shift in the air before I was up to my elbows and sucked...

-9.5-

...In.

Something had gone wrong. There was no sign of the future streets of London, the sharp lights and pounding sounds. I was on a beach, a long empty stretch of sand broken up by sharp grass dunes. It seemed familiar but, for the life of me, I couldn't put my finger on why.

"And just where the deuce did you suddenly spring from?"

I turned round to see a man dressed in old-fashioned clothes, Frock Coat and gold embroidered waistcoat. The whiskers on his cheeks were thick and his eyes deep set beneath bushy brows. I knew him, I was positive, his face was familiar but I couldn't place him.

"Who are you?" I managed to croak, sick to my stomach from whiskey and disorientation.

"Ha!" he exclaimed, drawing himself upright and rolling his thumb in the ticket pocket of his waistcoat. Then it clicked. Even before he spoke I knew where I'd seen him before. I'd never met the man but I passed him almost everyday. Well, the *representation* of him anyway: the bronze statue that had stood on Gravestown front for as long as I'd ever known it.

"I, young sir, am Joshua Walgrave, and you happen to be scrabbling around on my property!"

TEN

"Duckers is away with the fairies."

That's what her father had always said, sat in his world of pungent varnish and the memory of pipes smoked; rum soaked shag that he'd relished since his Navy days. She always remembered his hands, large and chapped with the dark brown grain of tobacco stains. She could watch him for hours, tucked away in a corner of his work shed, as he carved and spun at pine and oak. She loved seeing him dig the shapes out of the wood, trimming the fat, finding the potential within each piece of timber. She would lose herself in the shadows and cobwebs, the dust and grinding of saw. Sometimes she would close her eyes and drift, fade away to the inside places, woken only by the feel of those rough hands on her soft young cheeks.

"There she goes again," he would smile, "away with the fairies."

Sat in her front room, trying to calm her nerves with cigarettes, she wished she could find those fairies. Right now there was nowhere she'd rather be. Somewhere calm, somewhere that smelled of treated wood and pipe smoke, somewhere far away...

She'd tucked Jessica into her bed and, after checking the room for sharp objects, shut her in with a chair wedged under the handle. It seemed sensible; the fairies that Jessica liked to run away with having a fondness for spilled blood.

Number Thirty-Three seemed content for now, alternating between rocking quietly in Sandra's armchair and cooing at the moon outside her kitchen window. Simple pleasures.

Greg was...

Well, who knew exactly *what* Greg was doing, whatever it was she'd let him get on with it. She just hoped the decision didn't come back to bite her on the arse. Shouldn't she be trying to look after him or something? Like a responsible adult would. Yeah... responsible adult, she'd never really felt like one of those. She was just a silly girl who occasionally went away with the fairies.

Chance would be a fine thing.

Tea, that's what she needed. Something nice and normal, something to ground her, something that was a world apart from death, lunatics and a town gone mad. Wasn't that the British way? Blood and thunder on all sides? Get the kettle on.

Tea was a science to Sandra, an inherited attitude from her grandfather, a man of almost superhuman gentility who smelled of Brylcream and always changed into his slippers the minute he entered the house. He had taught her that making tea was something to be relished not rushed, warming the pot, spooning out the leaves, waiting patiently while it brewed. There was no haste to tea and anyone that thought so had no right making any.

Sandra liked tea.

Though sometimes it tried her patience.

-10.2 –

Paul Bosher was a distinctly unusual man, not only because of his predilection for amusing ties.

Though that certainly helped. Bright ones, sparkly ones, ones with cartoons on them; he had all sorts of unforgivable neckwear lining the back of his wardrobe.

But the main reason he could be deemed unusual right now was the fact that he had come to Gravestown on holiday. Ten nights in The Bolingbroke Guest House out of season and he wasn't even having an affair with somebody local. He was here - as he had been every year at this time for just over a decade – because he *liked* it. This marked him out as a very strange man indeed.

Not that he would be coming next year, of course.

He had become aware of something wrong with the town earlier than most. He had been stood on the front, gazing out at the rough waves, and just felt it, deep in his gut. He knew the place well, knew its atmosphere, knew its moods – that was, after all, why he came here. He felt in tune with the place – and had simply known that there was something askew. If you had asked him why he would simply have shrugged, maybe put it down to the loss of the twin girls, something his landlady had been only to eager to tell him about the minute his battered suitcase had touched her carpet. Paul Bosher was not a man prone to flights of fancy, whatever his dress sense may have implied.

He had carried on with his habitual pastimes, walking along the front, reading a book in the café there (he had, in fact, been sat only three tables away, watching Dallion construct his bizarre house of cards) and ferreting away in rock pools with the small net he always carried with him. There was nothing Paul liked better than crustaceans, you see. Well, crustaceans and rocks. Paul had a particularly fine selection of varnished stones, trophies from countless coastal haunts.

Through it all the niggling feeling of something wrong played on. When the girl reappeared he had accepted that would affect people's mood and, again, made rational excuses to himself. But still the feeling persisted.

Then, over the next three days, he had the bizarre fortune of passing events by a whisker. When lovelorn Lisa took a wet kiss from the clown on the front he had missed it by moments; struggling to sleep he had taken to strolling along the promenade to get some sea air in his lungs and, as he stood opposite The Anchor pub with a yawn on his lips she was giving away her eyes to the gullet of a nightmare. When PC Collins (aka 'Lola') took an assisted dive off the pier with a face full of makeup and gore Paul had been just around the corner, admiring a window display of fishing reels in the local tackle shop. He'd heard the shouting but dismissed it as youthful hi-jinks and kept his distance. As Karen Wright took the knife she kept for the Sunday joint and slipped it into her husband's mouth Paul had been stood right outside her house, admiring the particularly fine hydrangea that bloomed by her front door. Why, only tonight, he had been filling his face with some fine 'Giuseppe's' cod when, a minute's walk behind him, the bronze statue of Joshua Walgrave had taken to eating stray gulls and young lovers.

Paul was just one of the universe's bystanders; he was born to be on the periphery of things. Except for now, because the sight of a double decker bus pelting along the street ahead of him had finally caught his attention.

There was one other thing of relevance about Paul Bosher, you see, he drove buses for a living; that was who he was for forty hours a working week. And he knew a stray one when he saw it.

"That's not right," he said to himself as he watched the vehicle nearly lose control on a tight corner. "That's not right at all."

Paul Bosher was about to break his cosmic position, he was about to get *involved*.

-10.3-

Moon dance, moon sing, moon love...

Number Thirty-Three looked up at the insidious, beautiful, hateful, gorgeous moon and shivered a little. She could hear it. Hear the delicate poems it spun like spider's web into the ears of its children, hear its promises, its commands.

She dug her nails into the soft meat of her upper arms and screwed her eyes tight shut. She didn't want to hear anymore. She wanted to sing her own songs.

But still it insisted.

She let go of her arms, leaving little red crescents where her nails had broken skin, moon children, and pressed her hands over her ears.

They were gathering.

And they wanted her with them.

She could hear the woman making silly noises to herself while she made herself a drink, tried to focus on it, hold on to the real...

But the real had no place for Number Thirty-Three; it wanted no part of her.

And still the moon spoke on.

"Ching ching! Last stop for this service!"

Paul heard the young man shout as he jumped out of the bus and ran laughing towards the waves.

He'd followed the bus all the way back down to the front, just along from the pier. It hadn't been difficult, the bus may have been quick but it was also incredibly noisy and left a rather obvious trail of wreckage to follow.

Having no great desire to be part of that wreckage Paul kept his distance, sticking to the shadows of a service alley that ran alongside the 'Penny Palace' amusement arcade. He watched as the rest of the kids got off and wandered after the driver – who appeared to be holding an excitable conversation with thin air. He tried to hear what the lad was saying; the wind was blowing in the wrong direction, snatching chunks of the words away before they reached him but it seemed to be about waiting for others to arrive. The lad wasn't happy about this, ranting and raving to his illusory colleague. The others just sat down on the sand and stared into space, clearly not in full possession of their faculties.

Definitely time to call in the local constabulary, Paul thought, not a man to shirk his civic duties. He found it extremely unlikely that anything the young man said was worth taking seriously – he was quite obviously off his rocker – but there seemed no point in taking any risks; if there were more on their way then the Bobbies could nab the lot of them, job done.

Mind you, he dreaded to think what manner of folk might have the slightest inclination of meeting with this lot. They'd have to be a pretty nasty bunch.

The noise, like a car crashing in slow motion, came as soon as he stepped out of the alley and, looking up, Paul had the first inclination as to how right he was...

'One for the pot.'

Though what the pot could possibly get out of it was beyond Sandra.

She didn't hear Number Thirty-Three enter the kitchen but then the woman was still barefoot so it's no great surprise.

She didn't hear Number Thirty-Three pick up the wooden rolling pin from the sideboard either but the kettle was whistling on the hob and her mind was elsewhere so, again, it could hardly be called surprising.

In fact, she only became aware of someone else in the room at all when Number Thirty-Three's hand touched her shoulder, making her jump. Turning round to ask if the woman fancied a cup of tea the last thing she expected was to feel the shaft of her rolling pin crash against the side of her head. No, that really *was* a surprise.

-10.6-

Well, thought Paul Bosher, *there's* something you don't see everyday.

Which was, in all fairness, a somewhat ridiculous understatement. But then, the human brain is only programmed to deal rationally with so much and when faced with something beyond its remit – say, an animated bronze statue of a town's founder towering several feet above your head – it's liable to think all sorts of silly things. In fact, it could be argued that his brain dealt with it superbly. There are many people whose brains, on seeing something quite so bizarre, would simply shut down, leaving them staring blankly at the thing that had caused such psychological malfunction. It is to Mr. Bosher's credit that, through strength of self preservation or just the basic lack of imagination to fully accept what he was looking at, he kept a sense of awareness and took to his heels. It was this speedy flight that ensured his continued existence as the statue had been only too aware of what it was looking at and swinging its heavy metal fist with enough force to smash his head wide open. As it was the statue did nothing but paddle at fresh air and Paul Bosher lived to see more rock pools and wear even more ridiculous ties.

As he ran, however, he continued to fulfil his universal role as a spectator. It became clear that the statue of Joshua Walgrave wasn't the only surreal arrival at this beach meeting. The mechanised laugh of the clown automaton ran wild as it moved jerkily from within the shadows of the pier where it had lain dormant since the death of Lisa Thompson. It wore garlands of seaweed around its shoulders and its white gloves had turned brown with the dried blood of its victim.

The streets leading to the sea were no longer as empty as they had been on his journey down either, as various lost souls, child to pensioner, made their way towards the pier. Some were vacant, wandering glass eyed, the victims of some inescapable siren call. Others were almost feral, laughing or screaming as they ran (the number of these would almost double as the residents of the Cliff Tops arrived in town, as they were, even now, no more than a stone's throw from its borders).

Things were going dreadfully wrong in Gravestown, he knew that much. He also knew that it was a business he wanted no part of. Whatever was going on here wasn't for the Paul Boshers of this world. He just hoped he could get out of here fast enough to keep it that way.

ELEVEN

"There's nothing quite so humbling as the potency of happenstance."

I was sure that Walgrave was quite right; whatever the hell he was talking about. Anyway, even if he wasn't it would have been exceedingly stupid to tell him so, seeing as I was sat in the back of *his* carriage en route to *his* house. I may not have been much of a socialite but I at least recognised the inarguable rule of not disagreeing too forcefully with your host's beliefs, especially when, frankly, you've got nowhere else to go.

"I mean," Walgrave continued, fidgeting with his fob chain in a manner that suggested he wasn't quite at home talking to strangers, "imagine if I hadn't chanced along that stretch of sand during my constitutional, you, my lad, would have been wandering lost long past nightfall. Makes you wonder, doesn't it?"

Indeed it did, I assured him, it made me wonder *lots*.

"I can't believe your uncle would be so remiss as to allow you to make the journey on your own. It really is quite flabbergasting."

Hmm. Flabbergasting indeed, my flabber was well and truly gasted.

I'd told Walgrave that I'd been on my way to visit a distant relative in Southampton and that I'd missed my coach, deciding to make the journey on foot instead. A particularly lousy story but one that Walgrave was clearly too self-absorbed to recognise as such.

"Well, you'll stay the night as my guest and then I'll see you on the first coach Southampton bound tomorrow morning."

"It really is dreadfully kind of you."

"Piffle, it's a trifle. Besides, Mrs. Walgrave will be only too happy at the diversion, life gets a little... monotonous out here."

Little would change a hundred years down the line I thought, but kept it to myself.

The little carriage rattled up the hill towards Walgrave's house, the gothic shadow that, by my time, would be the asylum I'd left only a few hours ago. I looked out the window and pictured Dallion tumbling down towards the sea. I shivered and stroked at the crystal at my neck.

The carriage rolled through the large wrought iron gate and along the gravel towards the house.

All of a sudden there was the sound of shouting and several men appeared from the rear grounds of the house.

"What on earth...?" Walgrave checked his fob watch and sighed. "Oh, of course."

"Of course what?" I asked.

"Nothing to worry about, young man, it's just Number 12."

"Number 12?"

"Yes, he attempts to escape every day at some juncture; some people really don't know what's good for them, do they?"

I looked out of the carriage window and watched as the men started to gather, lanterns and clubs in hand. They were all staring upwards, shouting and pointing at the roof of the building. I looked up and, silhouetted against the moon, I saw a naked figure dart across the roof slates, long beard rippling behind him as he ran. He was skin and bone thin, moving in a frantic manner, like an animal. Behind him I could see two more men clambering out of the skylight he'd presumably escaped from. They stepped cautiously, Walgrave wasn't in the habit of hiring fools, and, even if he had he certainly didn't pay enough for heroics.

The lunatic began to laugh as the moon washed over him, running towards the corner of the building nearest the adjoining wall.

On the ground several orderlies began to gather, clubs and torches in their hands.

The lunatic didn't pause as he jumped from the roof, sailing three or four feet through the air to come landing on the top of the wall. I twitched involuntarily, imagining the pain, the jarring of the muscles, the rough brick cutting into his bare feet.

No sooner had he landed a net flew through the air, hurled by two of the orderlies on the ground, it caught him by the arm as they tugged and he fell back inside the grounds, dropping another six feet or so to the gravel. As soon as he was down the men piled onto him, beating him with their clubs or kicking him with booted feet.

I looked to Walgrave, expecting, naively perhaps, that he would stop the violence. He wasn't even interested, staring at the shadows from the opposite carriage window.

"Full moon tonight," he mumbled, fiddling once again with his pocket watch. "I wonder what's for dinner?"

- **11.2** –

This was a bad place.

There could be little doubt of that. Even excusing the natural distaste I felt for the place, both because of what I had seen outside and my experiences within its future there was enough objectivity left in me to know that it went foundation deep. It was everywhere, in its cold floor tiles and its thick wallpaper, its dark wood panelling and the leaves of its multitudinous pot plants. Even Walgrave, who seemed so innocuous on the surface, held part of it inside him; a shadow behind the eyes, a slight twitch in his left cheek. Something had happened here and it had broken the building and everyone in it.

The place didn't look all that different, the layout was identical, the decoration just a little fuller.

Walgrave had me escorted directly to a spare room on the first floor with the instruction that I should wash and prepare for dinner; frankly I was glad to be away from him, his lack of concern about the brutality towards Number 12 had sickened me and a little time to calm down would make it easier to remain civil.

The maid that had shown me to my room reappeared with a neatly folded selection of clothes that her master felt would fit. I wondered for a moment where the garments had come from before realising they had, no doubt, been stripped from some unfortunate's back as they were admitted to the place; inmates' cast-offs. It felt ugly, but I supposed I should play the game for now.

I looked out of the window at the familiar countryside

and suddenly had the very real urge to cry. How the hell was I to get away from here? Not the building, that would be easy enough; it wasn't bricks and mortar I was trapped by, it was *years*. I began to realise quite how stupid I'd been to try this.

"Can't really disagree with you there."

I was surprised by the sudden voice but determined not to let it show, I recognised it you see and wanted to be able to maintain a little decorum, a little strength of character.

"Worked though, didn't it, Charlie?" I said, turning round slowly to face the 'god' that had appeared in my room.

"No. It didn't. And I'm not a god, Gregory, I thought I'd made that clear the last time."

He looked a little different, fuller, less wasted. He was clothed too, a rather ungodly check shirt and jeans.

"What are you then?" I asked.

"The point is more what I *was*. You and I are not so very different. Normal folk caught up in things that should have always remained beyond us. Too much knowledge changes you, Gregory, the more you know about this universe the less capable you are of living normally in it, there are *things* out there..."

"More than this?"

"Yes..." he sighed, "and isn't that what always leads us astray? I jumped into my role, grabbed it with both hands, learned new abilities, and learned *everything*. Look where it got me. A hospital bed and a mind that won't be still." He looked at me, a rather sad look in his eyes. "They never tell you that in the books, do they? They never give you that one last chapter."

"What do you mean?"

"A wardrobe full of magic, a garden full of mystery, magical trees with doorways to other lands at the top of them; in the books that stuff doesn't affect people after the last page is turned. You really think you could just walk away from all that? Carry on with your schoolwork, your job, and your *life*? Of course not, you've been altered; collateral damage. Do you really want that?"

"Bit late isn't it? I mean, in the last twenty-four hours my world has changed. Completely. For better or for worse isn't really the point anymore. is it? Okay, maybe it would have been better for me in the long run had I never known, lived in ignorance of all this but... well, I *do* know, don't I? And frankly I'm just going to have to get on with it, what other choice have I got?"

Charlie sighed. "Dallion has a lot to answer for."

"So says the spectral bloke talking to me from the future. You're no better, mate. Now, are you going to be useful and help me out or what?"

He sat in silence for a moment, no doubt weighing the situation up with what he deemed suitably enigmatic gravitas, then nodded.

"It's all here, everything you need to know."

"Good." I started changing my clothes. "You can show me then, can't you?"

"If you're so determined to be a part of this you can find out for yourself."

"Bugger off." He was starting to annoy me now, and the shirt Walgrave had given me was itching like fury; too much starch. "I'm not having you come in here acting all concerned for my wellbeing and then wafting off because the conversation didn't quite go your way. If you're really bothered then you can prove it by helping me out."

He laughed, an actual, honest to God, trace of humour.

"Come on, I'll give you the tour."

There was hope for him yet.

-11.3-

"It all comes down to desire."

We were walking along the corridor outside my room, heading back towards the staircase. Well, *I* was walking at least, I noticed after only a few steps that Charlie's feet didn't quite touch the carpet – which, considering his immense abilities must have been a conscious decision, for someone that claimed discomfort about his godly appearance he didn't half play up to it.

"One of the most basic human emotions, a universal constant, everybody wants something after all."

"A brief explanation for example?"

It was good to see I was still capable of cheek.

"Life fills every space, follows every pattern, everything has its place in the scheme of things. I've told you that there are things outside of what you would know of as reality, creatures, beings..."

"Yeah, you mentioned it once or twice."

"Well they come in all different forms, solid, ethereal, humanoid...*other*. And they have varied needs, all dictated by what nature can provide. Anything of abundance will somewhere find a consumer."

"Somewhere a Waffle Monster must be feeling very full."

"Gregory!" Charlie spun around and growled into my face, "You demand my help and then you do your best to ignore it! Kindly shut your mouth."

"Sorry."

He sighed and carried on floating towards the staircase.

"Although you have put your finger on it at least, everything has its devourer, including desire. Now, there should be more than enough floating around to satiate their needs but it appears that something's getting greedy; stepping into our reality, interfering with things, altering people and events so as to create even more."

"You're telling me this is just about something pigging out? All of this weirdness is just to build the larder up?"

"Basically, yes. It's messing with the natural food chain, force breeding and genetically altering its prey so as to consume more and more."

"That's bloody horrible."

He smiled.

"You've got a surprise coming over the next forty years or so, but yes, you don't mess with the natural order of things unless you're willing to deal with the consequences. Of course, in this situation it doesn't have to, *you* do."

We started climbing the stairs.

"It began here, playing on the desire it found in one weak moment, and then spiralled out to your time, building more and more."

"Weak moment?"

"A single little tragedy, something that history would barely wink at, but something that was enough to turn one woman's life on its head."

We'd stopped outside a door; he reached out to the knob and gently swung it open.

I stepped a foot or so inside and then found I couldn't move. The room was pleasant enough, all white lace and William Morris wallpaper but the scene that was playing out on the large four poster bed robbed me of all sense for a moment.

It was a middle-aged woman, dressed head to toe in black. Her eyes were red from crying, her fingers red from blood. Surrounding her were the dead (please tell me they were dead) bodies of children. Slowly I recognised them, one I knew personally, the rest from the posters that had been pasted all across the town for the last few months.

"Gregory, meet Eliza Walgrave, a woman of great desire. The desire for children."

She looked at us and reached out with one damp hand.

"Please tell me," she whispered, "why do they never breathe?"

-11.4-

"Flotsam and jetsam."

He said. We were back in the corridor, Charlie resting one strangely substantial hand on my shoulder.

"She lost her own child when it was still in the cradle and it broke her mind. Now it brings her surrogate children, damaged children, feeding her need."

"But... why are they so... damaged?"

"Dragging something forcefully through time leaves its mark, there are ways – methods and avenues – to travel safely, it didn't bother to use them. All you're left with is pieces."

"Like the foot on the beach?"

He nodded. "A little piece of the game, a nudge to the Gravestown of your time. Presumably it returned Jessica for the same reason, to create fear, heartbreak, all good breeding grounds for desire. Everything it does is to create more emotion, it could have made the effort to bring them through alive – unhealthy perhaps, but alive - but it doesn't want to give her healthy children, that would fulfil her desire not feed it even more."

"Sick."

"Yes."

"I didn't mean... I..."

I threw up.

"Oh, right, yes... sorry." He looked away. "I'm afraid that's just the start of it, the real problem lies back in your time. Reality itself is unravelling; that doesn't come easily."

I did my best to tidy myself up a little, wiping at the corners of my mouth with my stiff cuffs.

"What has it done?"

"Reality is a fragile thing, you can nudge it a little, a bit of magic here and there, what you mustn't do, however, is punch a hole right through it."

He handed me a small photo in a frame.

"I took it off her bureau." It was the picture of a baby. "That's the key to the problem, a monumental change in the order of things. Fix that and everything else should fall back into place."

Touching it I felt dizzy, as if there was a slight current running through the frame. I heard a noise: waves, muffled, the lonely wail of gulls. I felt the world rock on the tide. I smelt salt, then something muskier, thick fabric, treated wood.

My eyes blurred as the corridor shifted, a patch of the house over by the stairway fading as a mirage appeared over it. The tides, a small boat with a man – Joshua Walgrave – leaning over the side, a small box in his hands, no, not a box, a *coffin*. He placed the coffin in the water and I watched as it rocked slowly for a while before beginning to sink.

"What did it do?" I shouted, trying to keep my voice above the ever increasing sound of waves, trying to keep my balance as the whole building swayed to and fro and the picture slipped from my hands.

Suddenly there was silence and the mirage disappeared.

"It didn't let her lie," Charlie said and picked the picture back up.

There came a crashing noise from the floor above, the splintering of wood and the sound of shouting.

"That's my cue to leave," Charlie said. "You'll manage the rest of the way without me, I think."

"You must be joking!" But he'd already vanished; the corridor was empty. Well, except for the naked lunatic with the long beard running screaming in my direction that was.

-11.5-

"You'll be Number 12, then?"

I said as he knocked me straight off my feet, landing roughly on my chest. I looked up at his animal face trying not to breathe in - he stank something rotten – and found my next piece of flippancy fade away. There was something in his eyes, something... The feral anger that had been there was changing, growing softer with confusion.

"Gregory?" he said.

Which was the last thing I'd expected.

He smiled and all of a sudden I saw even deeper, saw beyond the years, the beard, the madness and, as he started to cry, I stroked him on the back of his head.

"Please tell me you're wearing the chain?" he whispered.

"Yeah... yeah, I am."

He tore at my shirt and grasped the orange crystal that hung around my neck, then with a growl he pulled it free and wobbled to his feet, the chain hanging from his long-nailed fist. Behind him I could see several attendants with clubs making their confident way towards us. He turned to face them.

"What are you going to do?" I asked.

"Being a person of considerable patience and goodwill I'm fighting the urge to kick the sods' heads in. You might want to look away, just in case my natural gentility fails to kick in."

So saying, Dallion swung the crystal against the hard edge of a picture frame where it exploded in a wave of orange light.

It took years off him, and not just because it was a pretty piece of jewellery.

The change wasn't perfect; he didn't become the Dallion of a few days ago. It was clear that he had still aged, though maybe only ten years or so rather than the thirty odd that it had appeared. His body thickened, wasted muscle gaining tone and definition where there had been only loose skin and sinew. He gained a couple of inches, though whether that was actual growth or his spine straightening out the hunch and kinks that had been forced into it over his incarceration, I couldn't tell. His beard and long hair remained but, like the rest of him, it took on an extra life, becoming bushier and darker. As he turned towards me, a grin on his face, I noticed the most important change of all. It was in his eyes. Gone were the traces of self-pity, fear and madness - well maybe not all of the madness, there had been a fair bit of that there from the first day I'd met him, but it was a different sort of madness, it was the merry lunacy of a man who had nowhere near as much sense as he had lust for adventure.

The effect on the attendants wasn't quite as unearthly but it matched it for drama. There's nothing quite so pleasing as seeing the confidence fade from a bully. They had considered this easy fun, an opportunity to add an encore to the beating of earlier. Now, even as the orange light faded, they hadn't a clue what stood in front of them, the only thing they knew with any certainty was that it scared them witless. They ran; can't blame 'em really.

"Oh," said Dallion, his voice a little deeper than I remembered it. "Well, that was a bit of an anti-climax, wasn't it?" He scratched at his long beard and sighed. "Now, where's my bloody coat?"

Nudity opens doors.

We proved the fact a couple of times as we marched through the upper floors of the building. I'm not saying it granted us free rein of the place but on both occasions there was enough of a shocked pause from the staff in question that Dallion had more than enough time to make their silence a little longer lasting (introducing head to ornate vase and oil portrait of migrating geese respectively).

"So, are you going to tell me how you did that then?" I asked while Dallion rifled through the boxes of belongings we'd found in a storeroom on the third floor.

"A magician never explains his tricks." He pulled a particularly gaudy silk shirt out of the box he was looking in and scowled.

"Oh come on, that was a bit more than sawing the lady in half!"

"Not as sticky, granted. Get back."

I stepped away from the door as a couple of attendants ran past, no doubt following the rest of their number into the grounds (the general assumption seemed to be that any escapee would immediately leave the building, which was logical enough). Once the sound of their running had faded, Dallion reappeared from the pile of boxes he had ducked behind. "Anyway, I would have thought it was obvious."

"Oh yeah, absolutely crystal, I was only asking to pass the time."

"As sarcastic as always. I moved through time."

"But Charlie said you couldn't just move people through time." An unpleasant flash of the children upstairs burst into my head. "It damages things."

"Which would be why I spent the first five years on the edge of brain death, dribbling and burbling; precisely why they locked me up in here. When were you talking to Charlie, anyway?"

"No chance, you finish explaining first."

He sighed. "Fine. Leapt out of time, jumped back a few years nearly frying my brain in the process, ended up stuck here. Passed the time by trying to escape; it beat waiting for someone to rescue me. The crystal I gave you contained energy, mine to be precise, you don't live the lifestyle I do without learning to have a little insurance. Smash the crystal, soak up the energy, Bob's your uncle, Fanny's your aunt, when did you speak to Charlie?"

I told him, both about how I'd got there and what I'd learned.

"Fine, pan-dimensional nonsense, hunger from the dawn of time, blah, blah... One day I shall retire and grow begonias, just for a bit of excitement." He kicked the boxes. "I can't find my stuff and I don't mind telling you it's starting to annoy me a bit."

"Someone's probably nicked it."

"They wouldn't dare! Aha!" One of the boxes had spilled when Dallion had kicked the pile and the sleeve of his coat was hanging out. "Told you, my belongings know better than to allow themselves to fall into enemy hands. I only work with garments I can rely on."

He began to pull his trousers on.

"How are we going to get back?" I asked.

"Well, that's the problem isn't it? It's easy enough for you; your body's still sat in Sandra's room." He got muddled with his shirt buttons and lost the thread of conversation for a moment. "Erm... Yes, I'm hoping that using you as a focus I can ride back in the flesh without completely losing it. The amount of traffic should help. Things have been dragged between the two time zones a few times now, so with a bit of luck the passage should be easier than would normally be the case."

"And if not?"

"Well, I'm not staying here, I tell you that much. We'll have to risk it. Aha!" He pulled his hand out of his coat pocket and held up a knotted lump of jewellery. "Today just keeps getting better. Adopt the position, young man, let's get on with it."

I sat cross-legged on the floor while he moved over to stand behind me, separating out his necklaces and bracelets and slipping his silver ring onto his finger. It must have been having Dallion close by because I began to feel reality slip away, almost instantly becoming stickier, softer.

"Well, if this doesn't work, young Gregory..."

-11.8-

"...You'll be picking my grey matter out of her curtains."

We were back in the bedroom, back in the time of Coca Cola and 45s.

"See!" said Dallion. "Piece of..." He fell backwards and landed with a crash on his unmade bed. "God, but my head hurts..."

"Shall I try and find some aspirin?"

"An axe maybe, I don't think aspirin would touch the sides. I'll be alright in a minute."

I shouted for Sandra. Nothing. I walked out of the room and downstairs, calling as I went. I couldn't imagine she'd popped out for anything. I nearly missed the spot of blood on the floor of the kitchen. Nearly.

"Doesn't look promising does it," said Dallion who had walked in behind me.

"No, no it doesn't. What do we do now?"

"We could order Chinese; maybe have a quiet night in?"

I stared at him, not in the mood.

"Oh alright, let's save the day first, but I'm definitely up for chow mein when it's all over." He smiled, "Let's make plans!"

TWELVE

The problem was in the water...

... that much was clear to any with the slightest
sensitivity in these matters. It was in the out of kilter
flow of the tides, the way the water crawled further and
further up the beach as if reaching out to the dry land;
eager to swallow... to *consume*. Yes, the sea held all the
answers, anyone with an even basic knowledge of such
things would realise as much at a glance.

But these days very few people in the town had
sufficient sanity to care less.

The beach was filled with people, residents of both the
town and the asylum (joyous of course at this unexpected
night out). Fires had been lit, more through a need
to see something burn than to provide warmth. Some
were dancing, others were wailing, some still hankered
for the reassuring spill of blood and fought and wrestled
with one another until they got their wish.

Karen Wright was there, the moonlight making the
blood of her husband and children appear quite black
streaked across the front of her housedress and face.

Derren Bright, face pink from standing too close
to the flames of the Bargainrite Bonanza, was still in
a mood to celebrate his thirteen years on the planet
and he and the rest of his friends had found ample
amusement in torturing poor, drunk, old Joe Rigby.
The man was putting up a fight though, clutching a
tatty old sandbag to his chest which he referred to as
his 'love', claiming that he would do anything to protect
her. Young Colin Reilly and Mike Fowler managed to
get it off him eventually and laughed loud at the old
man's screams while they tore it apart.

Even one-time mayor, Arnold Newman, had decided
to show his face. He and the faithful Smithers were
roasting a few select portions of his most irksome and
termagant wife in one of the bonfires and very much
looking forward to the crispy results, smiles on their
faces and wet sheens to their mouths.

Jeremy was there of course, trying to ignore the
insistent demands of his older self wittering in his
ears and get back some of the sense of fun he'd felt

earlier. Eager Joan had turned out to be something of an easy touch, sharing herself freely amongst the gathered crowds and he fancied another go on her, if only to try and better his previous attempts. It was difficult though, his 'Guardian Angel' being particularly vocal by now. He watched the clown, sat cross legged in the sand, laughing as always, and envied it its simple pleasure; how glorious it must be to be happy with so little, to never feel the bite of 'want'.

Above them all the statue of Walgrave stood proud, occasionally swatting any foolish person that strayed too close but, for the most part, content to stand and observe, a proud father watching his children at play. Today was a good day, the start of a new – albeit brief – era for the town. There would be no more disappointments, no more false starts, the future was written and nothing – and nobody – would be able to change so much as a line.

"Good evening!" a voice shouted from the edge of the prom. Despite the chaos, the noise and distractions, most people stopped what they were doing and looked towards the man and boy that had arrived unnoticed. Some recognised them, the man's clothing was certainly distinctive and the boy had lived here all his life, but others hadn't the first idea about the new arrivals. There was no doubting the authority they carried, however; there was something intensely *heavy* about their presence.

"I'm overcome by the powerful desire to make sandcastles. Would there be anyone here willing to lend me a spade?"

Silence, except for the crackle of fires and the constant rush of the sea.

"No? Nobody? Dear oh dear, somebody needs to show you miserable buggers how to have fun."

And with that, the Magician and his young friend entered the fray.

There's never a policeman around when you want one.

This is - and probably always will be - a common truism, but for Paul Bosher, right here and now, it was also a deeply irritating fact.

Since running from the beach he had seen all manner of mad folk heading in the direction he was trying to flee from. He didn't know what was happening in Gravestown tonight but it certainly wasn't the sort of calm and easygoing local event he had attended on previous visits.

To make matters worse he was being herded back towards the beach. Try as he might, everywhere he went huge crowds of people were between him and safety. In order to try and avoid them he found he was constantly making his way back the way he had come, staying ahead of the lunatics rather than risk making his way through them. Which, though it made sense in the short term, really didn't seem all that sensible when followed through to its logical conclusion.

He had looked for somewhere to hide but, aside from banging on front doors – and who knew what might answer him in that situation? – he was distinctly short on options.

For the first time in his life Paul Bosher found himself wishing he'd gone somewhere else for a holiday.

"This can't be very sensible, can it?"

Gregory asked as one by one the residents of Gravestown stopped what they were doing and began to move towards them.

"Possibly not," Dallion admitted with a chuckle. "Exciting though, isn't it?"

"One word for it. I imagine the being pulled to death by lunatic mob part might take the edge off it, though."

"Nah... that's the best bit." Dallion stepped forward and raised his hands in the air. "Not going to happen though." He flicked his right thumb against the silver ring he wore and the central section begin to spin, slowly to begin with but then starting to build as some magical momentum carried the metal around. There was a high whistling sound and a small pulse of light flared from his ring finger. The whistling continued, not harsh, rather musical in fact, and, as he moved his hand the eyes of everyone on the beach followed.

"Okay," Gregory whispered, afraid to break the mood, "that's impressive, I'll give you that, but what do we do now?"

"Well, I stand here looking mystical while you hunt for Sandra and Thirty-Three."

"Oh. Don't suppose you fancy swapping that around, do you?"

"Not really, I'm good at being mystical, playing to my strengths, y'know? It won't last forever though, so I'd get on with it if I were you. They must be here somewhere."

"Fine, I'll just go and find the worst place to be stood when your Mojo packs in then."

Gregory moved slowly into the vacant crowd.

-12.4-

The most painful thing about being brained with a rolling pin isn't so much the initial blow, it's the coming to that really throbs.

Still, Sandra supposed – as much as she was really able to suppose *anything* with a drugged up colony of pain monkeys playing steel drums in her head – that the sheer fact of her coming to at *at all* should be seen as a positive and life affirming event and that to moan about it was somewhat missing the point. There had probably been a great number of people in history that never had the opportunity of appreciating the after effect of skull meeting solid object; a brief moment of 'what the hell was that?' and then no more. No doubt, had they had the mental capacity to do so, they would have loved to

171

be in her position.

No. Empathy be damned, her head was killing and she'd give anything to be blissfully unaware of the fact. Of course, the constant bouncing up and down didn't help, what was all that about? She opened one eye and immediately regretted it as the light of a street lamp above her shoved six-inch nails of pain into her forebrain. Still the bouncing continued. She really was going to have to take a look; maybe the pain would lessen as her eyes grew accustomed. She tried again. The pain *didn't* lessen but curiosity, followed by a dose of surreal appreciation, carried her through it for the three or four seconds or so she needed to piece everything together.

Okay, to take stock then. She appeared to be lying in a wheelbarrow that was being pushed down Gravestown High Street by a raving lunatic of her recent acquaintance. Yeah...you couldn't bloody script it, could you?

-12.5-

"She's not here,"

Gregory hissed.
"You're sure?"
"Of course I'm sure!"
"Oh. Well that's buggered that up a bit then, hasn't it?"

-12.6-

The sea was hardly deep blue nor was it really the devil on his heels, but the expression popped into Paul Bosher's head nonetheless as he saw the pier ahead of him.

A lot of people had gathered now (although the number would surely treble by the time everybody he'd seen on the streets found their way down here). The statue appeared dormant, at least for now. Still, things really were getting somewhat desperate. He needed a way to escape all this, get to safety somehow... but with half the town behind him and half...

Oh, well, there was that of course... risky, but in his current situation what wasn't?

-12.7-

"You had a plan, remember?"

Dallion flicked away the comment with his spare hand. "Yeah... well it relied on certain factors being in place which, so far, they're not. Frankly, at this point it's a little more freeform as plans go."

"Last time you said that, you ended up falling off a cliff."

Slowly, the sound from his ring was fading and the lunatics were regaining the little control of their minds they had in the first place.

"Yeah... you've a point there, maybe we should regroup."

The crowd began to circle them; no way out.

"Okay," Gregory whispered, "how about I meet you a couple of inches to our left? I can just manage to move that far."

"Hmm... not going well, is it? Now, if I'd been sensible and kept us apart, this would have been a great time for the one who wasn't surrounded by raving nutters to provide a distraction."

The sound of the bus engine firing up and the grinding of gears filled the beach and the crowd turned to see what was happening.

"God, I'm good," Dallion grinned.

-12.8-

Paul Bosher was to running what a slug is to Salsa dancing.

The two had always been mutually incompatible. If anyone who knew Paul Bosher had been there to see him sprinting towards the bus they would have assumed mental illness played a part. If they'd heard his laughter as he jumped on board they would have been absolutely convinced of the fact, perhaps rightly so. There was no doubting that some of his faculties were still in place, however, as he leaped into the seat and turned the engine over with one confident movement.

His laughter stopped as he realised quite how many people were heading in his direction but he held himself together and began to reverse off the pavement and onto the road. He had a chance to get away and he was damned if he was going to let anyone hold him back.

"Excuse me," a voice said behind him, coincidentally at the exact moment he remembered the rear door would be wide open, "any chance of two singles to safety?"

He turned to see a tall man in a leather coat and a young lad.

"Depends whether you're as mad as that lot out there," he said, pulling forward nonetheless.

"Oh abs..." The lad stamped on the man's foot.

"Just drive, please," Greg replied.

-12.9-

Knowledge can be overrated; it's all well and good to know you're in a problematic situation but it goes little way towards helping you out of it.

So, yeah, Sandra was being taken for a bumpy ride towards the front. What next? She supposed she should make some sort of attempt to escape, feeling as she did it was likely to end in disaster though, if opening her eyes was difficult then how much more complex would jumping from a moving wheelbarrow and fighting off her kidnapper be? Number Thirty-Three was clearly fighting fit...

"The moon's going to love me."

...if completely off her rocker (and tone deaf at carrying a song in Sandra's opinion, not that it was largely relevant). Perhaps she would do well to bide her time and assess her situation when she knew more about what the woman had planned?

"The moon's going to love me when I kill the silly lady!"

Oh...

"Thank you, driver, this'll do nicely."

"You must be bloody mad if you think I'm stopping this thing until we're a good few miles away," Paul Bosher replied, looking Dallion in the eye with what he hoped was sufficient determination.

"Pull over," Dallion whispered, with that same air of manipulation that Greg had seen before.

The bus drew to a halt. They were on a street leading from the front which was, thankfully, now empty, everyone who had been heading towards the beach having already arrived.

"So what do we do now?" Greg asked.

"Well..." Dallion moved to the back of the bus and gazed out of the rear window. "We wait for everything to get in place and then we save the world a bit."

"Number Thirty-Three?"

"For starters, yes. She's obviously keeping a lower profile than I expected. She's the core to all this so I assumed she'd be there with everyone else, but she must have other plans. I only hope she's not hiding away somewhere doing something unforgivable to Sandra. That would surprise me, this whole thing's been about spectacle, working the crowds, so you'd have thought it would carry on in the same vein."

"Nice to know you're still completely in control of the situation."

"Doing my best *given* the situation...I'm gambling that the creatures controlling her will make her perform some kind of grand gesture, some sick little piece of theatre. I could be wrong, she could be working her quiet way around the town slaughtering everyone she sees." He was getting agitated. "She could be miles away, spreading the pleasure. She could be out on the cliffs performing elaborate Japanese mime! She could be... oh..." He leaned forward, squinting out of the window. "She could be pushing the silly bint towards the pier in a wheelbarrow."

Greg followed Dallion's gaze.

"I can't see her."

"Eat more carrots, come on!" He dashed back to

175

the front of the bus. "Let's go and be in mortal danger again, it's boring sat here."

"What about him?" Greg said, pointing at Paul.

"Good point, off you get," he said, gesturing towards the door. "If all goes according to plan you should be perfectly safe out there."

"What if it doesn't?" Paul asked getting up and moving anyway, in a daze, all fight out of him. Dallion jumped into the driver's seat and glanced at the controls.

"Then you've no chance anyway so there's little to lose."

As soon as Paul stepped off the bus Dallion swung it into a three point turn, knocking Greg off his feet.

"Let's get this over and done with, shall we?" he shouted, barrelling back towards the front.

-12.11-

It was all getting too much for Jeremy Ashe.

His head was no longer his own, his heart had died and God help the state of his soul. He looked up at the pier and remembered the violence of earlier. It didn't please him as it had, now it just seemed an impossible event, something he couldn't possibly have been part of.

But he was. Dear Christ, he was.

And didn't he just wish the world would shut its mouth and leave him alone because of it?

He noticed a woman come running across the road towards the pier pushing something in front of her, and felt a surge of panic; something in him just told him that there was more blood on its way.

From over his shoulder he could hear the sound of the clown laughing as it drew close behind him. Ha, ha, ha...

He spun round and grabbed its wooden throat.

"Shut the fuck up!" he screamed, kicking and tearing at its body. "Just shut your stupid fucking mouth!" Its suit ripped and gelatinous seaweed spilled over his fists. Still he kept attacking, ignoring the pain of his left index fingernail peeling back as he scraped at its face. He lifted it up and ran screaming towards the closest bonfire. It laughed still as he shoved it into the flames, the heat searing his fists (he'd never play the guitar again now, even if he had wanted to), the noise only dying as the fire took hold of its face, paint bubbling, nylon hair fizzing.

He stood back to watch, aware that lots of people were staring at him.

"It's not fucking funny," he said.

From the road he heard the sound of the bus returning, quickly followed by the sound of the statue of Walgrave coming to life once more...

-12.12-

"Fly me to the moon!"

Number Thirty-Three screamed as she rolled Sandra through the open barrier and onto the wooden planks of the pier.

Sandra grunted as the change in surface threw her up in the air slightly and, as she came back down, she used her dead weight to spill the barrow. Number Thirty-Three gave a shout as the metal handles were torn from her hands and she went tumbling forwards.

Sandra tried to get to her feet but could barely move, the shock of being thrown to the hard floor sending waves of pain through her skull.

"Silly woman, silly woman," Thirty-Three mumbled through a split lip. "Silly woman, come here!"

She grabbed at Sandra's hair and began to pull her screaming along the floor towards the end of the pier.

-12.13-

"Have you ever driven one of these before?"

"No," Dallion replied, the rear of the bus swinging out and clipping a parked car as he turned onto the road that ran along the promenade, "does it show?"

"A little," Greg replied, pulling himself back onto his seat. "Please tell me I'm imagining the statue thing."

Walgrave was charging across the sand towards the

pier at a speed that was surprising, considering. It grabbed the edge of the pier and began to climb onto it.

"Pretty spry for his size, don't you think?" Dallion muttered, gunning the accelerator pedal and turning the bus towards the pedestrian entrance for the pier.

"What the bloody hell are you playing at?" Greg shouted, instinctively putting his hands in front of his face as the bus smashed through the ticket booth and glass fronted arcade.

"I am a man of magic, young master Ashe." The bus crashed back into open air, windscreen a mess of cracked glass, the sound of torn metal screaming. "A sorcerer and philosopher, a humanitarian follower of the left handed path..." The statue reared up thirty feet ahead of them, pulling itself onto the pier in a shower of splintered wood and metal. "I solve every problem I can using the sharpness of my mind, not the hardness of my fists. However..." He stamped on the accelerator even harder, the engine roaring at breaking point. "...there is only one viable way I can think of right now to deal with a magically animated bronze statue."

Walgrave opened its cave mouth in a silent shout.

"By twatting it with a double decker bus?" Gregory whined, dropping to the floor for safety.

"Yep."

The bus hit the statue square on.

-12.14-

Mad she may have been, but it would have taken more than that for Number Thirty-Three to let the sight of a bus hitting a living statue pass unnoticed.

She dropped Sandra and stared as the statue grabbed the front of the bus and both tore towards her, tearing the side railings from the pier as it went. The boy (Gregory, his name was, Gregory) jumped from the side door and rolled along for a few feet, eventually followed by the idiot, the man who had died.

The bus continued, its momentum too great to keep

it safe on the pier. Slowly its wheels inched over the side as the angle of its passage took it further and further from the line of the pier and, for a moment it hung there, the statue still gripping the cab. It moved, just a fraction, reaching its hand out, still desperate to squeeze soft flesh in its metal fist; it was enough. The bus toppled over the side and hit the water with a splash that carried far enough to fall on her shoulders. Glancing over the side she watched as the lights sunk down into the black sea.

"Moon dance," she whispered as the lights fizzed out.

Then Sandra swung her foot at her knee and things began to go a little downhill.

-12.15-

It's amazing what the body can do when pressed.

Sandra was white hot with pain but the fight or flight condition was strong and, beyond that, beyond the basic programming we all possess that brings out the best in us when our backs are against the wall, she was damned angry and that made her stronger still.

Thirty-Three dropped to the floor and Sandra kicked her again, and another, one to her rump and one to her shoulder.

"That, you bitch, is for trying to make me a damsel in distress," she grunted and put one more kick in while she still could.

"And what a delightfully demure damsel you are too."

Dallion was walking towards them, Gregory following on behind with a slight limp.

"Groovy beard for a dead guy." Sandra muttered.

"You like?" Dallion stroked it with a wink, "Surprised to see me huh?"

"I'm beyond surprise at this point, I'm also beyond being called demure, do it again and I'll tear your balls off."

"Bet Lancelot never had to put up with awkward sods like you," he chuckled and crouched down in front of Thirty-Three.

"Idiot," she hissed.

"Perhaps," he replied, a soft tone in his voice, "but I'm sorry to say I know someone who shouldn't exist when I see one."

He reached into his coat and, conjuror to the last, pulled out the large box Gregory had seen in his vision on the stairs.

"I'm sorry, Francesca Walgrave, but you shouldn't be here. You never had your time and this shell you've been walking around in is a cruel trick on reality, nothing more. Time to stop. Time to go back where you belong." He handed her the box.

As she touched it, the poor deluded dream of a dead child grown old shone brightly and disappeared, time papering over the cracks.

A ripple went out, the world shimmering and blistering as the real took over. Deep within the water shapes coalesced briefly, forced into form before being tugged away. The residents of Gravestown felt it, the insistent voices in their heads fading as the things from outside slipped back through the closing gaps in reality.

Jeremy Ashe looked down at his burned hands and began to feel the pain, wonderful and real, coursing through him.

Karen Wright saw the blood on her clothes and knew it for what it was and, with that knowledge, broke down in tears.

Derren Bright, birthday boy, looked down at the broken body of poor old Joe Rigby and felt a terrible need for his mother.

Dallion stood up and gazed out at the waves.

"And as for you!" he screamed. "You who think you can just play games with this reality, twisting and turning people until every drop of worth is wrung dry from them, well, who do you think you are?" He thrust his fist into the air. "Don't think this is the end of it, not for one *moment*." He slumped down and looked at the sudden quiet carnage of a town waking up to what it had done. "Not the end at all." He looked up at the moon, nothing but a reflective lump of rock, just as it had always been. "I'm *coming* for you," he whispered. "Get ready."

He turned towards Sandra and Greg.
"Let's finish this off, shall we?"

-12.16-

"What are you eating?"

Greg asked.
"Don't know," Dallion mumbled, throwing the barbecued meat back in the fire. "Something that old man was cooking for him and his dog." He grimaced. "It wasn't very nice."

They were on the beach now, a beach that was slowly emptying of people as they slunk back to their homes, back to warmth, normality and denial.

"I'm not going," Gregory whispered.

"What do you mean, you're not going?" Dallion replied, fixing Greg with a pair of the saddest eyes he'd ever seen.

"Just that."

"But it's not over," Dallion urged. "We've got to chase those things out there, hunt them down and finish this all off."

"No. *You* have. I can't go."

Dallion sighed and looked to Sandra who was on her feet now, head wrapped in a makeshift bandage of a torn shirt. She shrugged.

"Can you blame him?"

"But..." Dallion shook his head, "do you really think you can walk back to your old life, your family and your books, all those cheap dreams? You really think you can do that after what you've seen?"

Greg shrugged. "Probably not. But I can try."

There was a moment's silence, fat and heavy. Then Dallion sighed and turned towards the water.

He held out his hands and slowly the waves ground to a halt, as if frozen.

The sea was still.

"What about you?" he said, looking to Sandra.

"Oh I'm coming, pal," she said. "I wouldn't miss it for the world."

He held out his hand for her to hold and then looked back at Greg.

"Please," he said, "I don't want to leave it like this. It's, well, it's just *wrong.*"

"No," Greg replied, fighting to hold his ground.

Dallion nodded and began to walk out across the surf, Sandra by his side.

They stepped over the first few waves, then, as the sea began to flatten out a little they just strolled forward, getting smaller and smaller.

"Greg?" Jeremy Ashe said, coming to stand next to his brother.

But Gregory Ashe couldn't hear him; he was lost, watching one more miracle as Dallion and Sandra aimed for the horizon, aimed for elsewhere, for more than this.

THIRTEEN

There's nothing quite so limitless in human nature as its capacity for the lie.

In the days that followed I heard all manner of invented fictions, each an attempt to more plausibly deny what had happened than the last. There was talk of gas leaks, an outbreak of rabies (one local councillor went as far as to suggest a press attended culling of Samuel Clements beach donkeys until someone pointed out that not only was it out of season – and the donkeys were therefore stabled away for the winter some ten miles away – but that the press would hardly be likely to slap pictures of dead donkeys all over their covers), there was even a rather convoluted saga of a Nazi Brain Control bomb that had been unearthed on the beach and triggered.

In the end they went with the obvious solution of blaming it on the asylum, a breakdown in security – a willing patsy was found and bribed to admit culpability – that had seen some of the more dangerous inmates descend on the town in a wave of violence and destruction. It had been the more dramatic townsfolk's nightmare for years and, therefore, was embraced wholeheartedly. The fact that a number of the higher-ranking police officers had been involved in the chaos on the beach guaranteed that all of the right noises were made and the outside world was well convinced of the 'truth' of events.

Paul Bosher, a man with a sense of duty as great as his love of shellfish, attempted to make waves, selling stories of animated statues and unearthly goings on to some of the more sensationalist papers, but people will always veer towards the comfortable and he was quickly branded a crank and a troublemaker. He learned to keep his mouth shut; life was just easier that way.

After a while people actually began to believe the story. The asylum was closed down, its residents shipped off to alternative locations (many of them with a few more grisly tales in their files) and the building was eventually sold to a man who'd made his fortune from plastic coat hangers and who would spend many years fruitlessly trying to be accepted in any of the local pubs as something more than an interloper.

Whether or not the truth of that night faded from public consciousness, the scars stayed very real. By the time the season rolled around there were a lot of changes along the front. Many had sold up and moved on; new owners, new blood.

Jessica's parents were among the first, taking their broken child to a new word, a world where she stood a chance, however vague, of healing. Whether she did or not I couldn't tell you.

The clown was never replaced. An ornamental rockery was put there instead, presented to the town, ironically enough, by Arnold Newman as a commemorative tribute to his wife's sad passing. She had always been proud of her green fingers, he announced to the gathered press, and made a splendid show of tears that would have been believed by all were he not seen living it up in The Anchor no more than an hour after the cameras and notepads had gone.

Closer to home things were a little less jubilant. Jeremy never got over it, never talked about it either. From the little I did know about his actions of that night I'm not in the least surprised. He dropped out of school and left town at the earliest possible opportunity (one of the McGregor brothers got him a job on a travelling fairground and he jumped at it).

I was in my room as he left, tatty holdall slung over his parka, his hands shiny and pink. He stopped briefly in the doorway.

"Do yourself a favour," he grunted, "and get out of here the minute you can, this is no sort of place to live."

I nodded, not only to please him, I'll admit. Gravestown was far from comfortable for me and I'd already set my hopes on following his example when the chance came.

"Look after yourself," he said, and that would be the last conversation we would have for nigh on ten years. Not one for keeping in touch was our Jeremy, or maybe it just took him that long to get himself straight enough to deal with it.

As it was, it took me a few years to escape. As desperate as I was to turn my back on the place I was determined to see out school, after all, I had a future as a writer to build towards.

It wasn't until I earned myself a place at a University in York – studying English, naturally – that I finally got out of that house and town. I admit to naivety, I had thought that the simple act of walking away would make all the difference and, yes, it did help, but Gravestown came with me, or a little piece of it anyway. In fact it always has.

I moved on, like many did. I studied hard, and played hard, but there was always a little drop of the sea in that one pint too many, a little salt air in that pot smoke. I met a girl, Jenny, who idolised Bowie and was fascinated by the occult. Long dark hair, wore a lot of black. She was a Sandra clone and I'm happy to admit it.

Of course, we didn't last. This one didn't walk off into another existence with an enigmatic street magician but she did fall for a Taoist plumber from Leeds. The end result was the same.

I'm pleased to say my affair with York lasted a little longer. After graduating I ended up writing scripts for a local tour company (soul sapping stuff but it paid enough to keep the lights on) and, aside from brief visits home, I ended up in Yorkshire for the next twelve years of my life, writing hack work by day, fantasies by night. As predicted, the writing began to take over a little, a few published stories to begin with then a few scripts for television (nothing grand I assure you, although I am the man who wrote the episode of Emmerdale where Seth impersonated Elvis. Yes, proud doesn't begin to even cover it).

That's how I met my wife actually. She's a masseuse (actually she prefers the term Massage Therapist - it sounds better and doesn't suggest hand jobs are on the menu) and was working on set when I finally got them to let me visit.

We fell in love, I got rubbed a lot. Can't complain really. I even get on with her kids (two by an earlier marriage). Really get on actually, they're important to me. Life was good.

And, when *The Imagineer* came out it got better. Not much, it was never the big success that Dallion had suggested. I still earn my money by doing corporate stuff rather than fiction, but people liked it. It meant something to them and, really, that's all any writer can ever ask.

There was one person who wasn't so enamoured. It was a month or so after the launch when he turned up. I was sat in my little office, smoking too many cigarettes (another hang on from Sandra I suppose) and trying to make a story about Hemingway and ghosts work.

"I could sue you, you know."

"Hello, Charlie, I wondered if you'd show your face."

He hadn't changed. I supposed that chronologically at least I had yet to meet his physical self, so maybe that's not surprising (I write fantasy but time travel still confuses the hell out of me). He was holding a copy of my book, flicking through it, a wry smirk on his face.

"Half of this never happened you know," he said.

"It did to the kids that read it."

"Yes, I suppose so. Life's all fiction in the end."

He left then, presumably having fulfilled his enigma quota for the day. Haven't seen him since.

I did meet one other person though...

-13.2-

"Pick a card."

It should have surprised me I suppose, but when you've seen the stuff I have, things rarely do. It's one of my most irritating features; at least that's what the wife tells me from time to time.

I'd come back to Gravestown to check up on Dad; since Mum left he'd vanished more and more into that obscure world of his and, although he was clearly happy, it made me feel better to check he still had some touch with reality from time to time.

"You're all grown up," Dallion said as he sat down on the bench next to me and looked out to sea. He shuffled his cards and with a flick of his wrist they vanished.

"You haven't, I'm pleased to see," I replied, giving him a smile.

"Can't see the point," he admitted, lighting a cigar. "So, do you regret it?"

"What, not coming with you? Every day of my life. I think about it when I wake up, spend the whole day with it at the back of my mind and then dream about it when I sleep. Doesn't mean it wasn't the right decision though."

"We won."

"Good, I wouldn't expect anything less." I smiled.

"You could come now, if you like. There's still so much you could see, so many places you could visit. It's a big existence out there."

I thought about it, of course I did.

"Nah, ask me again next year."

"What? You? Happy with your little life? Your small house, wife and kids, mortgage and microwave meals?"

"Yeah." I looked at him then and saw that same look of sadness I still remembered seeing on a beach, all those years ago. "Because it's *magic*. Now shut up and let me buy you a cup of coffee."

He smiled.

"Alright then."

And I did. We talked, he told me about Sandra – she'd taken to the life of an inter-dimensional adventurer very well apparently, although she found the fact that Rothman's weren't as readily available in some existences as others something of a bind. I told him about Debra and the kids, about the excitement of surprise birthday parties, Christmas mornings and lazy nights with a bottle of wine and a good movie. And, as I talked, I began to realise something.

"I've got what you want, haven't I?" I said, stirring two sugars into my Grande Cappuccino – no frothy coffees and milkshakes on Gravestown's prom anymore, oh no, the world had moved on.

"Silly, isn't it?" he sighed. "Two men with just enough knowledge of the other's life to lust for it. We always want what the other's got, don't we?"

"Yeah," I admitted. "You know what I think?"

"No."

"The best thing," I smiled and took a light from his finger for my cigarette, "is just to get on with it."

So we did.

MORE THAN THIS

Guy Adams collects careers like baseball cards. In his, surprisingly limited, time he has tried his hand at Museum Curator, Tour Guide, Historical Researcher, Newsagent... Seriously, he needs working on that boy.

His main occupations however have always been acting and writing. In the former he has mugged people in *Emmerdale*, watched Rugby in *Where The Heart Is*, perved around in his Y-Fronts simulating sex with a woman dressed as a horse (Genet's *The Balcony*) and earned something of a reputation by impersonating real people (Hemingway, George Bernard Shaw and Hitler to name but a few). He also toured as one half of the wittily titled Adams & Jarrett on the comedy circuit and is the youngest actor to portray Sir Arthur Conan Doyle's Sherlock Holmes professionally.

So there.

As a writer he has churned out scripts for the above comedy shows, falsified Elizabethan Mummer's Plays and works as a columnist and reviewer for Canadian Theatre E-Zine 'The Boards'. That's when he's not crowbarring every conceivable genre or style into one novel to make absurdist word soups like *More Than This* or the *Deadbeat* series.

www.guy-adams.com
www.humdrumming.co.uk

Other Titles by Guy Adams
Deadbeat - ISBN 1-905532-02-4
Deadbeat: Dogs of Waugh - ISBN 1-905532-14-8

Also Available
The Imagineer, by Gregory Ashe
FireEye Edition - ISBN 1-905532-01-6
SnowScape Edition - ISBN 1-905532-00-8

DEADBEAT
BY GUY ADAMS

ISBN 1-905532-02-4

"I think you're missing something, what did you notice about the woman in the coffin? ...She was breathing. Not a common habit amongst the dead."

It's the middle of the night and, in a dark suburban churchyard, a group of men are loading a coffin into the back of a transit van.

But why would you be taking a full coffin away from a graveyard and, more importantly, why is the occupant still breathing?

The matter obviously needs thorough investigation by the best, most capable authorities.

Which is a pity as the only two witnesses are a pair of drunken ex-theatricals with reasons of their own to avoid the police.

Tom Harris (nightclub owner) and Max Jackson (habitual barfly) are on the case.

God help us...

...a world away from the bloated procedurals that have come to dominate the crime field, harking back to a time when fiction could be quirkier and less boundary-conscious. Tell a good tale, be scary, be funny... easy to say it, much harder to pull off. Deadbeat manages all three."
STEPHEN GALLAGHER
Author of Oktober, The Spirit Box and Valley of Lights

Deadbeat is the first in a series of adventures set in the secret underbelly of contemporary London, a place where the dead walk, magic can be bought on street corners and anything is possible.

Frankly, it's just like every other Pulp Crime/Horror/Zombie/Comedy/Thriller you've ever read.

Deadbeat : Dogs of Waugh
By Guy Adams

ISBN 1-905532-14-8

"High on life..."

There's a new drug running rife amongst the Undead community. Once ingested it simulates all of the symptoms of the living, faster pulse, perspiration, the intoxicating rush of blood through your veins...

Not that Max or Tom would be stupid enough to try it of course, they're far to busy smashing their senses to a pulp working their way though Deadbeat's new cocktail menu.

But when people start vanishing from the Soho streets and some of their customers disrupt big band nights by keeling over dead for the second time they decide it might be worth looking into, if only to stop profits dropping too far.

Which, in a lifetime of bad decisions, may rank as their worst yet.

Deadbeat: Dogs of Waugh *is the second in a series of adventures set in the secret underbelly of contemporary London, a place where the dead walk, magic can be bought on street corners and anything is possible.*

Frankly, it's just like every other Pulp Crime/Horror/Zombie/Comedy/Thriller you've ever read.

THE IMAGINEER
BY GREGORY ASHE

ISBN 1-905532-00-8 - SNOWSCAPE EDITION
ISBN 1-905532-01-6 - FIRE EYE EDITION

"If it were that easy, we'd all be heroes"

This is not it. The world you know - normal, safe, boring - is just a stepping stone to other worlds, other places. Places of magic, monsters and limitless imagination.

Like most eleven year olds, Charlie Whittaker always hoped this was true. Now he knows it is.
Because somebody's kidnapped his Uncle and he's forced to give chase.

Leaving normality far behind...

He will make friends on the way: the enigmatic Lashram, the absurd Squintillion, the noble Algernon. He will see sights that will make the wildest dreams of his life seem bland.

But will he survive long enough to enjoy them? There are horrors out there, ravenous cannibals, lethal assassins and, of course The High Lord Jethryk – a man who wears shadows torn from his victims and could snuff out all life in the universe using no more than his smooth fingertips. There is, in fact, only one power Jethryk doesn't possess, a power he intends to steal from Charlie's uncle.

By whatever means necessary.

It's all about story you see, and the power of imagination, one false word and creation as we know it will cease to exist...

The Imagineer *is a beautifully illustrated novel that hearkens back to the child in all of us, a modern fairytale that will excite older children and adults alike. There are other worlds to explore: sometimes wonderful, sometimes terrifying, always spectacular.*

All you have to do is believe...

THE OPENING
BY JAMES CHRISTIE

ISBN 1-905532-03-2

The world spins, mankind goes about its business sure and certain that all is well.

Nothing ever changes, day follows day follows day.

Mankind is so very wrong...

Moving from the mountains of Andalucia to the black ghettos of the Mississippi Delta, from a mysterious encampment in the Negev Desert to the Oaken Groves of Britain's High Druids, Colin Mage, modern day magician, races against time to prevent The Opening... A magical ritual that opens the gates to Hell on Earth.

Even with the Help of people like Michael Fry, The Merlin of Britain, Helen Ross, the Wiccan Priestess from the Scottish glens, Herschall the Jewish shaman with powerful political allies, John Light, one time Satanist turned evangelical Christian and Leon Shapiro, the Mossad agent who has more faith in guns and computers than in mystical beliefs, the odds appear insurmountable.

It is Castillo, an isolated village in Southern Spain, that becomes the battleground for the final conflict between Man and his greatest adversary, and it is only in Castillo that Mage discovers who his true friends are and the appalling extent of his enemy's capacity for pure evil.

FIRE OVER KABUL
BY LEO KESSLER

STORMTROOP EDELWEISS ARE BACK!

It is 1942. The height of the Second World War.

Germany's fearless elite reconnaissance and assault
company, Edelweiss, are now back in thrilling action. Under
the personal orders of Reichsführer Himmler, Edelweiss CO
Colonel Stuermer leads his troops from Kabul, in neutral
Afghanistan, across the treacherous mountains of Nepal,
through the dark rain forests of Assam and into the heavily
fortified British Raj.

If successful, the mission will herald the Nazi
'liberation' of India.

Aware of the danger, Stuermer commands Stormtroop
Edelweiss all the way.

Himmler knows that with their courage and experience,
Edelweiss are the only troop that can complete the mission.

Stuermer knows that, with one false step,
the mission could be their last...